FROM THE CAVES

FROM THE CAVES

a novella

Thea Prieto

2019
Red Hen Press
NOVELLA
AWARD

Red Hen Press | Pasadena, CA

Book design by Mark E. Cull

Library of Congress Cataloging-in-Publication Data

Names: Prieto, Thea, 1986– author.
Title: From the caves : a novella / Thea Prieto.
Description: First edition. | Pasadena, CA : Red Hen Press, [2021]
Identifiers: LCCN 2021013362 (print) | LCCN 2021013363 (ebook) | ISBN 9781636280028 (trade paperback) | ISBN 9781636280035 (epub)
Classification: LCC PS3616.R5376 F76 2021 (print) | LCC PS3616.R5376 (ebook) | DDC 813/.6—dc23
LC record available at https://lccn.loc.gov/2021013362
LC ebook record available at https://lccn.loc.gov/2021013363

The National Endowment for the Arts, the Los Angeles County Arts Commission, the Ahmanson Foundation, the Dwight Stuart Youth Fund, the Max Factor Family Foundation, the Pasadena Tournament of Roses Foundation, the Pasadena Arts & Culture Commission and the City of Pasadena Cultural Affairs Division, the City of Los Angeles Department of Cultural Affairs, the Audrey & Sydney Irmas Charitable Foundation, the Meta & George Rosenberg Foundation, the Albert and Elaine Borchard Foundation, the Adams Family Foundation, Amazon Literary Partnership, the Sam Francis Foundation, and the Mara W. Breech Foundation partially support Red Hen Press.

First Edition
Published by Red Hen Press
www.redhen.org

"In the illogic of myth you can find prefigured the big bang theory of the origin of the earth (Hawaii); the expanding universe (Navaho Indian); the origin of life in stagnant water (Dahomey, West Africa)."

—Penelope Farmer,
Beginnings: Creation Myths of the World

FROM THE CAVES

CHAPTER ONE

Sky hears no talking when Green leaves the sea cliffs. All he hears is the fog net snapping in the offshore wind, the whine of the plastic fabric as it tears from its poles and unravels across the glass-littered beach. It is only with his arms jumped into the whirl, fingers clawing at the airborne net, that Sky notices a fleck of movement high on the distant bluffs—a falling dot. It sprouts legs as it slices the dark cliff face, knees skimming the sheer rock, two feet diving toward tide pools heaped with boulders jutting. The shredded net tugs loose from Sky's grip as the dot silently grows into Green, and Sky wants to grab, wants to speak, but all he can think is I am seeing this, No—but I am seeing this happen.

A palm slaps red to Sky's face.

Pay attention, yells Mark as he stomps the netting flat, into a ground alive with stinging sand. Further down the beach Tie kneels on the uncoiled fabric, her kinked fingers humming the threads back together, and Tie and Mark have their heads low, they are still working—what do I do? They didn't see it happen, what do I tell them?

Then the rapid beating of footsteps—Teller runs open-mouthed past the net, kicking up slivers of tin, his empty water bucket clanking to the ground. Eyes snap up the bluffs to Green's unattended bonfire on the summit. When Mark and Tie drop the net and start running down the beach, Teller is already knifing through the surf, almost to the tide pools.

At the churning base of the cliffs, the suck of low tide holds pockets of noise—a hissing wind, the boom of brown ocean waves. A distant shout from Teller. Up ahead Mark and Tie leap the broken mounds of asphalt, Teller so tall he crosses in strides, but Sky still needs both hands to climb the tables of salt-split cement. The bubbled rock bites his fingers, Sky's toes are soon raw and raked, and when the back of Mark's head dips out of sight, the clouded morning sinks huge, suffocating, and Sky is alone. The shallow whirlpools gulp louder, the dirty froth spins faster—keep moving. The others are just ahead, breathe, breathe, can't breathe, the world is hungry, the others have left me, Green's gone, he's dead, the World—giant and alone.

Sky's bare chest scrapes from heart to navel as he scrambles to the top of a concrete slab, back into the ocean roar, and suddenly below him are three sets of naked shoulders—Mark, Tie, and Teller crouching low in the tide pools. Half-hidden in their circle, a tangle of red arms. One purpled knee crooked outward. Pale hips flattened against a mat of plastic trash.

Please, Teller begs Green. Tell me.

Under Tie's floating hands, the corner of Green's forehead is red against the rocks. One of his green eyes is open, the other closed. His bearded cheeks are spotted with sand.

Tell me, Teller shouts at Green. Tell me the stories are true.

The ocean rumbles. The tide rises into Green's open eye.

Say something, whispers Teller.

A wave swells rank foam over Green's chest, and Tie grabs at Green with sharp fingers. She shakes his shoulders like she might wake him from sleep, lightly at first but then urgently, fiercely, her mouth dragging a rough inhale that coughs into a crackled moan. When she pulls one of Green's limp hands to her cheek, against her flaked and whispering lips, her round stomach hugs against her knees, swaying, and the fear in Sky's chest boils to his face—hot, painful sobs. Green teaches Sky how to swim in the ocean and helps him build the fire. Green knows about evaporation jars and water filters and surviving the long, quiet summers. He's the one who calls tides by their color and knows where to dig for roots and makes Tie laugh when she's hungry and tells stories to stop the Dark Sickness but Green, Green—what will we do now?

Mark stands, his hands atop his head, and glares up the sea cliffs at Green's smoking bonfire. His fingers slowly pull into thick fists, gripping clumps of his matted hair.

Stupid, says Mark, and Tie chokes quiet. Mark ducks

for a chunk of cement and pitches it with his whole body at the shadowed bluffs.

I told you it was a stupid idea—

Don't call him stupid, screams Tie.

Green fell, says Sky.

Stay out of it, Waste.

Mark, it was an accident, says Teller. Green lost his balance.

Because the wind's dangerous up there, doesn't anyone ever listen to me? And he hadn't eaten in three days—

That wasn't his fault, yells Tie. This isn't his fault.

One look at Mark's angry face, his scrunched nose and sun-bleached eyebrows, and Sky closes his eyes. He blocks out the sight of Green's ear bleeding into the surf, but even as the ocean crashes and groans, Sky can still hear Mark's slicing words.

Green cared more about that bonfire than he did about taking care of his own teeth, that's why he couldn't eat anymore.

Mark retches a sob. His voice cracks into a shout.

He would've burned up our whole firewood supply and risked all our lives for nothing.

Be quiet, Mark. It's the only way to signal the others.

There are no others, Teller.

The wind leans against Sky's shuddering body, an empty, lonely weight.

We have to fix the fog net, says Mark at once.

When Sky looks up, Tie and Teller are staring at Mark,

both frowning. Mark's narrow face is tight but dry, gazing south beyond the gray crescent of the beach and its heaps of melted plastic garbage, past the sand dunes piled high to the black-mouthed caves in the headlands. The caves, thinks Sky—safety, escape, Home—but far off a murky cloud is rearing across the red mountains inland, a tower of dust swallowing the jagged ridges, chewing its way closer.

We need to fix the fog net before the storm hits, says Mark, his voice flat. We need to put out Green's fire and save whatever firewood is left. There are so many things we need to do now that—

—now that Green is dead? shouts Teller, and Tie yells against her clamped lips, clutching her stomach tight. Stop, Mark, just stop. We need to slow down, we need to talk about this.

With one light finger, Tie wipes the sand from Green's forehead. The gesture is intimate, private. Sky averts his wet eyes but Mark's words ramble, his fingers shaking and counting.

I'm sorry but it's already summer, every day the fog net catches less water, and without Green we'll have to work harder than ever—

How can you talk about work right now?

Tie, I'm talking about water, for you and Baby.

Tie drops forward onto her palms, her large belly hanging. Spit drips from her twisted mouth, lips silently forming Green's name.

Teller jumps up like a fist, and though he's the thinnest of them all, knob-spined and basket-ribbed, he's taller than Mark, taller than Sky on his concrete perch. His dirt-stained hands clench as his hairless chest expands wide. When Teller speaks, his dark-circled eyes stare at no one.

That bonfire was more important to Green than food or water, says Teller, and Green taught me to remember the dead above everything else. I'm taking his body to the fire.

But we could push him out to sea, says Mark, confused. His body will be poison soon—

Green always honored the others.

It's too dangerous up there, the storm—

Mark, you're either going to help me—

—no time for traditions—

—or you aren't.

Teller picks cautiously around the red-stained rocks and tangled rebar, and slips his hands under Green's shoulders. When Tie lifts Green's thin ankles, his broken pelvis lengthens purple at its joints, his right side hangs low, so Sky drops down in the tide pools near the others and wedges a shoulder under Green's sinking thighs. The skin of Green's legs is cold but pliant where Sky wraps his arms, stiff where his ear presses against Green's hip. The stink of seawater and urine. A familiar body sweat smell. A moan weeps from Sky's mouth.

A heave and they lift Green's body together just as the tide surges, the ocean growls, and Teller's toes fumble the wet rocks. His heel drives into a knot of rusted metal shingles, and when Teller's foot reemerges, a dangerous red shows through a slice in his foot wrappings.

It's nothing, Teller says to Mark's widened eyes, quickly adjusting the wraps to cover the wound. When Mark steps forward he hisses Stupid under his breath, folds his long arms around Green's chest, and they all move toward the beach.

As they cross the sand without speaking, Sky can feel the lurch of Teller's limp, Tie's shuffling steps, and the pop of Green's hipbone. He tries to focus on these sensations instead of the gathering weight of Green's still legs, to ignore the fog net cracking in the wind and the empty water bucket rattling down the beach. Instead of the spinning heat and his dry tongue, he focuses on the path directly below him, on the ankle-deep dust that, as they climb the sand dunes, then rest, then climb the bluffs, hardens into stone steps and ledges of burnt brick. Their path tightens as they approach the blackened basement of One, Two, Three—the structure with one standing wall and three intact windows—and the trail swings near the cliff edge at Three, Two, One—the hole where a house crumbled into the ocean in perfect thirds. Near the top, where the cracked cliffside leans into the air, Sky and Teller have to change positions to fit through a snarl of pipes and steel beams pulled low by their collapsed foundations. They pass puddles of melted pitch and finally emerge onto the exposed peak of the bluffs, and by then Sky's naked body is burned and rashed. The charging wind rocks his steps unsteady, the heat blurs his vision, and the cool touch of Green's skin relieves nothing of the red afternoon sun.

At the brink of the precipice, in its deep, circular fire pit, Green's bonfire smolders low. Thin trails of smoke rush in all directions, but Green pegged enough splintered plywood nearby to raise the flames again. They lower Green's body into the crater of coals and shining tar and heap the entire stack of wooden planks over his head and torso. Though Mark mutters about saving the floorboards for their own firewood supply, he helps push coals over Green's dirty feet, his scarred hands, and every part of Green is covered when the mound ignites.

I would like to say some words for Green, says Teller when foul brown smoke and the smell of burning hair push Sky low to the ground. Tie crouches as well, her muddy eyes closed against the rising ash and slashing wind.

Mark opens out pleading palms to Teller.

Teller, says Mark, we worked hard to bring Green up here. It was a good thing to do, I admit it. I think Green would've appreciated it, and he would've agreed that we have to leave now.

Teller stares hard past Mark's hands, takes a deep breath and continues louder.

I want to tell a story about Green, which is also the story of why we're here.

This is stupid, shouts Mark. The storm's coming in.

It was Green's ritual, he deserves a eulogy.

No time for stories—

Would've made time for you—

—need to be smart—

What we need is—

—water and food and firewood—

—I'm the oldest now—

Stop fighting, do you hear me, stop it, yells Tie and she's on her feet. She stabs a coal-blackened finger at Mark, then at Teller.

Mark, speak or shut your mouth and stop interrupting Green's story. Teller, let Mark speak so he can go away, if he wants to leave so badly.

From behind the smashed brick wall where Sky retreated, he watches Tie stand with her big, square hands on her thin hips, her hard stomach distended. Mark shies from her rigid frown, bowing his head.

I didn't mean I want to go back alone, says Mark.

The planks in the bonfire shift and sparks whip the lip of the pit. Mark's eyes flick to the storm, which has already clouded and consumed their path home to the caves, and his jaw muscles twitch. He finally lifts his hands toward Green's body to speak, stretching his fingers wide in the traditional way.

What I mean is, says Mark, Green was my friend, too. He helped me after Mother died, and he taught me hard work solves everything. He was always happy when he was helping people, but cold and distant when he told all those stories about a past that wasn't real—or even if it was real, couldn't help us anyway.

Teller frowns and shakes his head. As the wind quickens, the bonfire rumbles and the bloody sun overhead drowns in a reek of ashy clouds. Sky curls himself into a ball to protect his skin from flying dust, and Mark also cringes, raises his voice, speaks faster—

Green knew we sacrificed time, sacrificed food and water when we told stories, and we'll be forced to make even bigger sacrifices right now if we can't move on without Green. I can do some of his work, but fixing the fog net and collecting water, I can't do those things alone—I don't want to do them alone.

Sky glances at Tie, at her body shot upright, her feet fixed and hands hanging at her sides, as though she can't taste Green's oily smoke in her mouth, doesn't feel the cutting dust. Her sharp jaw clenches as it always does when she's angry, but her eyes are also so wide, so empty, that Sky wants to slip his body under her arm. He wants to press his face against her smooth, curved stomach, against the quiet heartbeat within, but Mark will only tell him to stop being a baby. Sky crawls closer to Tie without touching her, and Mark kneels a short distance away, his hand shielding his face from the smoke.

When Teller steps close to the fire, his long fingers are already aimed over Green's body, gesturing into the wind. His voice deepens until it rolls clearly under the whistling air. It comes loud, from low in his stomach, easy and slow, the way that makes words vibrate in the cave tunnels, the same way Green tells stories—

—told stories.

Heat tightens Sky's face.

I would like to talk about the path that led Green to this moment, says Teller, lengthening his words. I would like to talk about his stories and his beliefs, and I would like to start by telling the story of Abraham, which was Green's favorite story.

Mark scowls. He glances at the storm crawling across the ridgeline, at Tie's attention absorbed on Teller, then flings a rock over the cliff and into the blinding dust.

When the Great Fires began and Moth flew into the sky, says Teller, every camp wandered in search of sustenance. When the Great Fires began and Moth flew into the sky, there were many people in this area and the blue ocean waved with green kelp and sparkling fish. When the Great Fires began, the wooden homes around the bay had not yet burned and boats arrived with jarred food to share, but after the Great Fires began, the wind stopped blowing the air free of ash. The fires spread, the storms grew, and the Enemy Ocean awoke. The camps grew in favor of finding another place to live but Abraham spoke, because Moth had flown into the sky. Abraham had gray in his hair and there were worry lines across his forehead.

Sky knows about those lines. Even as the wind threatens to roll his body, as he clings his fingers into the cracks in the ground, Sky remembers seeing those lines between Tie's eyebrows, around Green's mouth. Worry lines, whispers Sky.

Abraham campaigned the camps, says Teller, and he advised everyone to remain near the sea. He said there's an Observatory right here, on this very spot we stand, that speaks to Moth. He also spoke of desalination and the condensation of coastal fog, said that the Seven Seas were the Seven Wells, but in the end he was not elected by the people. The majority went into the desert and have not been seen since.

A boom in Sky's ears—the storm bursting against crumbling walls of burnt corrugated tin. Both Tie and Teller crouch as sand is flung up the cliffs, lifted all the way from the beach. The squall of dust surges against the bluffs, and although Teller is still speaking, his voice is no longer a steady hum.

Listen to me, shouts Teller with an arm crossed over his face.

Mark and Tie watch the dark storm overhead.

I believe Green's stories are true, shouts Teller. Song told us the same stories, stories passed down to her by other Tellers. Green told us about when the first cave tunnels were built, so people could live underground during the summer. He knew when the boats stopped arriving at the beach and the insects disappeared—

Another boom. Nail heads pop at Sky's feet as tin sheets rip from frames and warped shingles fly over the cliff edge.

Teller, let's go, yells Mark into the wind.

Teller continues louder.

Green knew when the gardens began to fail and driftwood became scarce, but he said, through all those times, Abraham sacrificed firewood on the mountain. Green couldn't have known—it happened long ago, before the Enemy Ocean rose and clawed into the cliffs—but he still believed. He kept the bonfire lit, so people might return from the desert, so Moth might find us. Green fell from these cliffs today while working for something he believed, and I believe he lived a life full of determination and hope.

Tie makes a choking sound and tears roll down her chin. When Sky reaches over and takes her gritty hand, her fingers squeeze.

There was much more we could have learned from Green, says Teller, but we can still learn from his stories. It's because of his determination that we should maintain the bonfire and sacrifice part of our firewood—

There isn't enough, yells Mark. Do you have any idea—

Must give meaning to our lives—

—need the supplies—

—no point in living if—

You're both acting awful, Tie shouts into the wind. Green didn't even like stories with fighting unless the stories taught us how to avoid it.

The windstorm blasts stronger, and Sky moves closer to Tie. Even behind her body's slight windbreak his skin burns against the speeding dust, and Teller retreats back from the fire as a column of sparks swirls into the air. Ash lifts from Green's flames, showing two blackened feet. The clouds above whirl close and dark.

We need to leave now, shouts Mark with lines on his forehead. Not anger lines, thinks Sky, worry lines.

Tie glances at the cliff edge, then at Green's blazing fire, and nods her head. Her grip on Sky's shoulder is hard as she leads him down the bluffs, Mark and Teller close behind them, and through a brief gap in the storm's flying dust and the brown smoke from the bonfire, Sky glimpses the bay stretched below. The lower slopes of the dunes and the long, gray beach are divided by a crosshatch of sand-clogged streets, canyons of ruptured asphalt, the metal crusts of automobiles, and blankets of garbage arranged in a sprawling block pattern. Brick chimneys rise out of tangles of fallen rafters, the frames scorched black, hollowed by fire and wind, the structures long ago skinned of their lumber by human hands.

And with the stench of Green's fire and the waiting stillness of the landscape below, Sky cannot imagine the cool sea breezes and blue ocean from Teller's story. As he climbs across the dunes and back into the quiet darkness of the caves, Sky wishes he could see the floating green and sparkling things Green liked to describe, wishes he could imagine people traveling by land and sea, but it's easier to remember sadness, thirst, and hunger when the ocean is an endless expanse of brown waves, a wide desert of seawater broken only by the distant, half-submerged remains of Old City. Out to sea, the torn shell of a single skyscraper and a lone section of a bridge loom out of the white-capped breakers, and the empty windows facing the beach are only sightless squares to Sky. Even though low tide reveals the flat tops of road signs and the hollow heads of street lamps, without Green the only meaning Sky can summon from the past is remote, quiet, and small.

CHAPTER TWO

Wake up.

Another nudge—Mark's foot prodding his shoulder. Sky blinks but everything remains dark. It is early.

Wake up, we're going to the net, says Mark, and Sky slowly coils his legs underneath himself. His outstretched fingers recognize the cool, hand-chiseled walls of the cave, and his toes know their way from the grooves carved into greasy stone. He orients himself in the blackness, head ducking the low ceiling of rock, but his first steps bump him into Mark's bare chest.

Mark shoves him backwards.

Get some plastic, what are you thinking, Mark hisses.

In the dark, Sky strains his hearing past Teller's snoring to Tie's breathing, and although it's been tens of days without him, Sky instinctively seeks Green's sleeping breath. Only four of us now just four, Sky scolds himself, as he smothers the sharp memory of Green's single open eye and reaches for the plastic cords Tie wove the day before. The buttons of his fingers feel past Tie's flinching knees, accidentally brush against Teller's injured foot. Teller yelps.

Hurry, says Mark, the sound of his footsteps shrinking into the tunnel. Sky follows the soft beat out of the narrow sleeping chamber, into the main passageway where he can stand at full height and hear the shushing of ocean waves around the dim entrance of the cave tunnels.

Outside, on the lower slopes of the bluffs, a fine sea mist collects on Sky's skin. The air steams against his face and the thrill of it, the dream of moisture, a moment later raises the hairs on his neck. The marine layer is lifting, burning off—morning is only a red stripe behind the shadowed mountain ridge but the heat will wake fast and thirsty. Sky trips down the sand dunes, passing quiet houses with black doorways and dodging the rusted bumpers of tilted automobiles. When he arrives out of breath at the beach, Mark is already at the fog net, one hand pulling the torn edge of the fabric taut, his body crouched awkwardly over the bucket and water spigot.

Fix the net, orders Mark, and Sky reconnects the ripped strands to the pipe base, redirecting the dripping fabric to the water trough and allowing Mark to focus on the thin dribble trickling out of the spigot. Once Sky attaches the last threads in place he runs down the beach, circling the entire length of net the way he has seen Mark circle it before. He slides his palms high and low along the netting as he goes, so the dew will accumulate faster and drip into the trough, and his eyes search every pipe connection for leaks. Since Mark is watching, Sky also quickly repairs minor tears in the net with Tie's cords while ignoring the more time-consuming rips—the fog has all but evaporated from the brightening sky and the hot wind is increasing. When Sky returns to Mark's side, the sun is already winking pink over the bluffs, slicing the top of his head with heat.

They both look into the bucket at the shallow puddle of water.

Tomorrow we'll take the net down for the summer, says Mark and they fall quiet. Their dark reflections move across the surface of the murky fluid, two triangle faces on a glowing background, Mark's shadow the larger of the two. As Sky watches the image ripple, the light glints to match Mark's clouded pupils, the pale scar that runs the length of Mark's peeling nose, and the frown he wears when he looks Sky's direction, if he looks at him at all.

But when Mark lowers the bucket, he is not frowning. The crease between Mark's eyebrows is relaxed and his high-boned cheeks are soft because his hairless chin isn't squashed sour. When Mark speaks, the round muscles of his arms are slack instead of standing and angry, and his voice is calm, not stinging, not hurtful at all. Every patient word from Mark pours glowing liquid into Sky's chest, and when Mark looks half-blind into Sky's face, he still believes Mark is watching him, really looking at him—he is actually seeing me at last.

I want you to filter this water, says Mark, his foggy stare holding. Teller's foot is getting worse and soon Tie will be too big to move around very much. I'm going to need your help.

Sky nods eagerly and with their faces close he can tell how similar their features are—the shallow bridges of their noses, their heavy eyelids, like thumb-smears of clay. Although Mark's eyes are gray and hazy, both of their right eyes have a matching droop and their wide-arced eyebrows hitch high. As they march up the sand dunes together, their footsteps matching as well, the invitation to join, to be near and included, still floats quietly in the air, and Sky's thudding heart makes his knees shake.

The morning heat has already pounded the air to waving when Sky follows Mark into the dark mouth of the cave, keeping the pulse of Mark's footsteps ahead of him and his fingertips outstretched to the uneven stone walls. Blackness soon presses up to his nose, a damp chill covers his sweaty skin, and after ten paces Sky feels a cold yawning pass him on his left—the entrance to the tunnel that leads to the deeper sleeping chambers. Another ten paces forward with the walls narrowing inward—a splinter of kindling from the firewood pile pokes his left foot—and then Sky turns right into the oldest, tallest tunnel that leads to the storeroom. Daylight flecks the ceiling and reveals the high cracks in the rock overhead, the fractures that jag up to the surface, and Sky's eyes adjust to the dim pink beams that brighten swirls of dust. The air in the tunnel is warming with the heat of the day and Sky and Mark's combined breath, but the floor's mix of brick and scored stones still feels cool underfoot.

Then the tunnel walls widen beyond Sky's reach, he

ducks again into complete darkness, and he knows he has reached the storeroom. He freezes in place with his arms still spread. No babies allowed, Mark always warned him, so Sky waits quietly on the brick step that has been permitted to him in the past, his senses perked to the upturned dirt nearby, the dense smell of water—the damp of growing things. He can also hear the padding of bare feet and fingernails scratching rock, Mark's movements quick and sure even in blackness. He navigates the important room with such ease that Sky's eagerness dips, and a moment later—a blink of light. A brick slides out of the far wall and into Mark's orange-lit palm. The open rectangle of sunlight falls across the rows of large water drums, the chipped clay pots, and glints against the edges of glass jars stacked to catch evaporation. A peeling shard of mirror next to Sky helps jump the light across the room, and when he squints he can just see the small hand-drawn scratches in the clay of the opposite wall, the long and detailed counting marks.

Don't touch these, says Mark, gesturing to one row of drums with cracked plastic lids. This water's already filtered and separated and it's ready to be boiled. All the new water goes in this barrel and—don't step there—

Sky jumps back from his first step into the corner of the storeroom, and Mark drops to the ground, feeling the dirt where Sky's foot landed. A long quiet while Mark examines the squashed soil, his thick shoulders bunching, and when he stands his hands are on his hips, his face glaring at Sky who stands nervously, disappointed—I've made a mistake already.

Where you just stepped, yells Mark, is where all the summer roots are planted. See, that's the barrel that leaks, it goes on top.

It was Green's idea, adds Mark, his voice quieter.

Another moment without speaking except now the silence is heavy and leaking. Sky is almost grateful when Mark points out the scratches on the wall and begins explaining the different columns and tallies, when his voice has regained all of its familiar bitterness. Mark's words clip off the stone ceiling, driven down into the top of Sky's head, and he doesn't interrupt Mark even though he already knows the symbols for counting days and seasons from the other tunnels. Sky doesn't know, though, the system for tracking the tides, the firewood supply, the water per person, the shredded tarps they use for washing, or the digging schedule.

As Mark speaks, Sky's attention trails up the lighted wall, following a long line of square-shaped dots and fingernail-sized indents. Up close he can finally see the line of dots continues to the ceiling, filling the high walls and winding all the way around the storeroom—hundreds and hundreds of small arcs and loops. In the hardest, oldest clay, where the walls are propped by iron beams, the dots are not dots at all but tightly gathered and overlapping markings, an intricate pattern of grouped scratches. Each tiny figure is different than the one that follows, a string of shapes increasingly more complicated and interesting and exciting.

What are those? interrupts Sky.

Don't you know what writing is, says Mark.

Sky ducks his face.

What's it mean?

Mark tilts his head to the side, itches his scalp.

I know what these mean.

Mark points him to the other side of the room, where the long pattern tapers sharply to just a few short strings of figures. There, above a heap of corroded metal coils, the square dots are not intricate at all, only plain, blunt punches in the clay.

That means Tie's name, says Mark, squinting and pointing at a single dot with eighteen indents next to it.

And that's Green's name, says Mark picking out another dot. The twenty-five scratches next to his name means twenty-five years.

Sky's ribs clutch his jumping heart, and he suddenly wants to lean across the water drums to trace Green, his name, his age, although he's sure Mark wouldn't allow it. Instead, he shapes the word Green in his mouth while looking at the imprint, moves his teeth and tongue as though Green might spring from this small, hushed language.

But only his own memories live in Sky's garbled sadness, of Green spending time alone in the storeroom, Sky peeking unseen from the tunnel, cautious not to disturb him. Time to think, Green called it, his body half-hidden among the supplies, back shaking with prayers and sobs as his fingertips traced the walls. And this scratch, thinks Sky, his fingers raised toward the clay—this scratch is Green's name, it belongs to him. Green's voice, his determination and hope—they are supposed to be here, stamped in the storeroom, but the plain dot does not even hold the jagged and painful fact of Green's death. It is only a spot, a depression. No detail, no voice, no memory at all.

Mark points to another dot on the wall.

And that's Mother's name, he says, and Sky shies from another dangerous past. He quickly notices, though, two other names in a line below hers, one name with sixteen indents next to it, the other with nine indents.

So when names are close, does that mean family? says Sky, the words skipping unguarded from his lips.

It doesn't matter, frowns Mark, turning away. Stop asking so many questions.

So that's your name, says Sky, pointing. And that one's mine.

You know nothing about family, Mark snaps, flipping around so fast Sky stumbles backwards into the dark shapes of the room. One of his hands plunges through a cracked lid into a water drum, a loud splash, warm drips down his arm, against his chest, and Mark is screaming.

Waste, he yells. You'll kill us wasting water.

Sky runs from the storeroom, his naked shoulders scraping the sides of the tunnel, loosening sand to the floor. In the main passageway, he trips over the firewood pile, retreats deeper into the cave's narrowing void, between out-crops and overhangs of rock, but Mark's words still echo.

You killed Mother, you'll kill us too.

At the end of the passage, where the tunnel ends in fall-en boulders, Sky grips the steel poles that support the re-maining roof of the cave. His rashed shoulders burn inward as his face burns outward. There is water on his face and on his hands, his salty crying mixing with the water from the drum, ruining it, ruining everything—I don't deserve to have anything or anyone, Please, only to please you, Mark, my brother, will I always be this way, a scratch, a dot?

It is a long while before Sky's breath slows and he realizes there are faint sounds at the other end of the main passageway—Tie and Teller's voices. As Sky crawls closer to the orange entrance of the cave, he can see the shadowed outline of Teller sitting against the wall of the tunnel, his legs stretched out before him. Tie shakes her head while she untangles a large knot of wires in her lap, unknotting and straightening, handing the wires to Teller to braid into ropes, and Teller whispers something too quiet for Sky to hear.

Don't talk like that, says Tie to Teller. Not all fevers are bad.

Teller tries to shift his weight, the unbraided wires in his lap move as one, and he grits his teeth.

It hurts more today, he says. What if it's metal poison?

What do you want me to say? snaps Tie. You'll get bet-ter. You have to get better. You're the only one who tells

Green's stories like he used to and I can't lose those too, I can't.

Teller doesn't move, wrapped in the fog of Tie's angry sorrow, watching her hands jerk the wires straight. When he lowers his head, Tie's face twitches toward the shadows.

Sky, is that you?

With her ear turned to listen, Sky edges from his hiding place, trying to keep his wet face and arms hidden. As he draws near, he can see the stiffness flexed through the coarse hair of Teller's leg. The wound on the sole of his foot has shrunk to a red crater, but his toes clench and the muscles of his injured leg stand and churn. Today his eye cavities are tunnels in his sweaty face.

Sneaking in the dark, says Teller, his voice friendly but hoarse. He smiles with a clamped jaw.

Was that Mark shouting, asks Tie.

Sky bows his head.

What's he angry about this time.

I spilled water, Sky mumbles, and Tie drops her wires.

Just a little, adds Sky quickly.

We count every drop, says Teller. Every drop is vital, Sky.

Vital, thinks Sky, like a beating heart—living patterns in clay.

Are the dots in the storeroom vital, too? says Sky.

You mean our names?

Sky nods, and Teller's eyes widen into pools of sparkling oil. When Teller nods, slowly, heavily, his voice is low and serious.

The most vital, Sky, more vital than any number or year. Those marks symbolize your story and my story, all of our stories, and Green's especially. Green always remembered and honored the memory of those who are—

Stop, interrupts Tie, her fists hovering on either side of her pursed face. Don't say another word about how he's gone, I can't bear it. Talk about something else, anything else.

A still moment. Dangerous memories crowd underneath Sky's prickled skin. The Dark Sickness opens its eyes.

I'm sorry, Tie, says Teller at last.

The wires in Tie's hands tremble before she looks away, toward the bright entrance of the cave. At the far end of the tunnel, the sunlight is a crooked triangle of waving heat, blurs of gray sand and orange light, and the rippling writes a brief and silent language in the air that does not comfort Sky.

How about a story, then? says Teller gently, looking from one unhappy face to the other, his voice reaching through the darkness.

No one moves for a long time. When Tie finally runs a thin wrist under her nose and sniffs wet, she holds out her arm to Sky—an invitation to come close. Next to the hard wall of her round stomach, her warm skin met first by his bare ribs and then his pressing ear, Sky curls up small enough to make her large belly his friend. With the warmth beaming off her skin, the fleshy smell and Baby sleeping inside, for a moment he forgets all of the ugly words Mark spoke, the hundreds of quiet dots in the storeroom and his hungry, crawling sadness. He wishes for writing with complex markings, words that are lovely and lasting.

How about the firewood story? asks Teller.

That's my favorite, says Tie.

Yes, I remember. Do you remember the firewood story, Sky?

Sky grins at the easy memory. He heard Green tell it many times.

Teller flattens his palms in his lap, the way he always does before a story. He sometimes nods at the ground with his eyes closed, the same way Green used to end his stories, but Teller always begins with his eyes open, his words directed into the toothed ceiling of the cave.

Well, if you want to find the best firewood in the world, you have to know where to find the oldest, strongest tree. But to find the oldest, strongest tree, you have to first find the oldest, strongest man.

What was he like when he was young? asks Tie. Sky smiles against the tight skin of her belly. She asks the same question every time, and he's glad he's not the only one asking questions.

When the oldest man was young, says Teller, he was tall and strong just like the tree, and he had a black beard all the way down his chest.

Tie quickly pinches the thin wisps of dark hair on

Teller's chin, and her stomach bounces under Sky's ear as she laughs. Her high-crinkled laughter ends, though, with the sound of Mark's echoed movements in the tunnels. Teller glances in the direction of the storeroom but continues his story, now looking at Sky with steady, teaching eyes.

The oldest man was also very smart and brave. He had a scar on the side of his nose from one of his more dangerous adventures, and although he grew angry and said hurtful things sometimes, he had a good heart.

Sky cocks his head. The oldest man never had a scar when the story was told before.

Tie whispers as Mark's footsteps approach, her words cupped near her palm.

Teller, you forgot the part about his storytelling, she says. That's the best part.

Teller smiles warm and fills the cave ceiling with pulsing words, his voice low and measured like Green's used to be. This, thinks Sky, this is a gift from Teller and Green.

The oldest man also had a deep voice, says Teller, and it was sometimes strong but mostly gentle, like wind in the trees. When the world grew dark, the oldest man would sing stories to himself, and one day the Evening Goddess noticed and fell in love with him. From the Garden of the Gods, the Evening Goddess wished for the oldest man. She would listen to his stories and sigh.

Tie sniffs wet again.

Out of the cave's darkness, bleeding into view as brown,

orange, and then yellow, Mark stalks forward with a water jar in his hands. A good heart, Sky reminds himself, noting Mark's scarred nose, but Sky still creeps into the covering shadows as Mark approaches and passes the jar into Tie's open palms.

He can't have any, says Mark, jerking his head in Sky's direction.

Did he spill that much? says Tie.

He shouldn't have spilled any.

It's too hot today, says Teller. Sky won't be able to help you if—

I don't need his help.

You do, insists Teller. We all need to help each other.

If I need help now, shouts Mark, it's his fault, anyway. Mother knew how to do everything and he only makes my work harder—

Don't be stupid, says Tie. No one's born knowing everything, not you, not Sky, not Mother.

Tie's hard eyes make Mark glance away. He picks at the ground as Tie stares down at her belly, frowns at it, and then examines the half-empty water jar.

No water until tonight, she says finally, and Sky knows speaking will only lengthen the punishing talk. The moment she decides, though, Sky's lips crack dry. His mouth feels coated with dust. As Tie tips the jar toward her peeling lips, grains of sand move in the charcoal-clouded fluid, and Sky can almost feel the quick liquid soaking his own tongue, rolling down his own throat. Teller is handed the jar next, and Sky imagines the word Water as a swirling bowled mark on the wall, simple and full, but with the others turned away from him the word also feels shallow, lonely.

When Teller finishes the last dirty dregs of the water, he coughs his raw throat and directs his voice into the ceiling again. He continues the story with his eyes closed.

The Evening Goddess, says Teller, fell in love with the oldest man. One night she appeared to him. She told him if he found the apple in the Garden of the Gods he could live forever and they could be together always. The apple was guarded by a snake that would kill anyone who came near, but the Evening Goddess promised to trick the snake—

You're telling the story wrong, says Mark. The goddess kills Snake, remember? She gets the apple and the oldest man gets to live forever and they are happy for many, many years.

Mark smiles at Tie, and Sky feels sick from the word Forever. The word sounds like darkness stretching, tensing.

Teller's chin lowers level with the ground, and his sweaty face glints orange in the light of dawn. He continues the story with his eyes still closed, his voice loud and deep.

However, the oldest man got to live forever but he didn't get to be young forever. Years went by and the oldest man grew small and wrinkled and gray, until eventually he became so small and wrinkled and gray that he became a little jumping creature named Grasshopper.

Abandoned by the Evening Goddess at a very old age and wanting to die, Grasshopper traveled to the Cave of the Dead, the place where the dead rest, but because Grasshopper had outsmarted death for so long he was taken to the Inferno. He was pulled down through many burning caves and tunnels, where the awful dead scream without sound, all the ghosts angry and sad and unable to confess.

Confess, thinks Sky, as Teller's words vibrate into the tunnels. Sky shapes his tongue around the word. It feels old and pretty—slippery. He imagines the word written long and looping in clay. Confess.

Grasshopper went to the deep center of the Inferno, says Teller, and there, in a small scalding cave with nothing but darkness and boredom, woke Toad, the hungry God of the Dead.

Grasshopper, said Toad, I will swallow you whole unless you tell me the beginning of the living world.

So Grasshopper remembered his songs from when he was a man, and he began to sing his stories. He sang about Walking Stars crossing the night sky and the Garden of the Gods sinking under floodwaters. He sang about people who spoke words of many different meanings, and about the many dead people who were piled into a few deep holes after. He sang about empty hands of every size and color and the complicated power of words on paper.

Toad frowned, disgusted by Grasshopper's dreams of a world worse than his Inferno.

Grasshopper, said Toad, I will cook you in oil unless you tell me the history of the living world.

So Grasshopper remembered again his old stories and

sang of times gone by. He sang about the ocean growing angry, the plants rolling up small and gray. He sang about powerful people who grew rich and quiet, and about poor people who grew hungry and angry and many. He sang about electric talk covering the world, the land growing old and tired, and the Walking Stars stretching out of reach.

Rich, thinks Sky with his eyes staring. The word feels like Plenty. It feels like More. The opposite of hunger—a popping fire Sky tries to draw in the dirt. Full, spiky writing. Rich.

Toad forgot his hunger hearing Grasshopper's songs, says Teller quietly. The living world seemed far more terrible than his Inferno.

Grasshopper, said Toad, I will bury you in stone unless you tell me the future of the living world.

So Grasshopper sang his last song, his voice growing as soft and as gentle as wind in the trees. He sang the story of Moon and Bear, which was the first time the story was ever told, and when Grasshopper's voice grew loud and strong, Toad began to sing as well, though he did not know what the story meant. Darkness came when Toad sang stories he did not understand, when death jumped loud and excited and inspired.

Inspired. Inspired. Sky repeats the strange, glowing word in his mind to remember for later. Inspired. Inspired.

Because Toad was inspired, says Teller, he allowed Grasshopper to return to the living world, and when singing Grasshopper leapt by all the ghosts, they began to follow. Toad also allowed this, but he shouldn't have. Stories are only meant for desperate living things, but more and more ghosts caught up to Grasshopper. They rose out of the Cave of the Dead and into the living world, a cloud of jumping creatures that turned the sky black. They became a locust plague as large as a storm, spreading across the world—

What's a locust plague? interrupts Sky.

The others flinch.

Quiet, says Mark. I'm tired of your stupid questions.

Since the story is coming to an end, Teller's eyes are lowered to the floor of the cave. Sky's words are soft next to Teller's deep voice and Mark's bite, but the words grow large in Sky's mind. They make his skin bumpy. His tongue burns. It itches with questions.

Why can't Sky ask? says Tie to Mark. A locust plague is a sickness that—

But Tie stops short. She squints at Teller for the answer, and then starts straightening her wires quickly. Teller's forehead wrinkles.

That's just how Green told the story, answers Teller. The story ends with the locust plague destroying the living world, then the Garden of the Gods, the apple, everything except the oldest, strongest tree. That's why only Grasshopper, who's still somewhere today, knows where it is.

The stories—they usually bring blurred dreams of other worlds, colorful thoughts that ripple the painful ones, but this time Sky has ideas, questions, deep scratches of words. The others stare toward the mouth of the cave, at the moving yellow heat of late morning, and after a moment Mark waves his hand toward Sky like he's pushing the questions away.

But even Mark's irritation does not stop Sky's thoughts. The words are in Sky's mouth. They are slippery. They are Rich, Inspired—Confess. More words spill forward. They come out asking.

What do trees look like? asks Sky.

Tie looks again at Teller's face. Mark clears his throat while watching Tie, and then opens his fingers outward in front of himself, like he's pulling images out of the air.

Trees are tall, says Mark, and they're made of firewood.

They grow in gardens? tries Tie.

Used to grow in gardens, says Mark.

So there used to be gardens, Teller says. There used to be trees.

The burning wind in the tunnel hums.

Sky asks, what's an apple?

CHAPTER THREE

In the dark throat of the tunnel, Tie's blistered palms stick to Sky's shoulders. He can tell by the way her fingers burrow into his bare skin, then relax, then burrow again, that Tie is lowering to a squat, wobbling back on her heels. His thin legs tremble to help balance her weight, her fingernails ordering him to keep steady as her large stomach presses against her knees. He finally hears water falling on stones, feels hot sprinkles on the tops of his feet. A sour smell.

Thank you, says Tie when she finishes, though her words are sharp. He heaves backward to rock her body upright and says nothing that might click her impatience, grown barbed and sudden in the core days of summer. Her arm crawls his shoulders as they step wide, over their compost and bucketed waste, and slowly she leads Sky out of the low pit of the tunnel.

As they climb over the rutted rock in the slim passageway, the light from Mark's fire grows brighter ahead and the dark outline of Tie's body takes shape—her enormous belly, her shoulders slumped into her deepened, stomach-propped breasts. Sky notices how her tangled hair has become darker as her stomach has grown larger, like it is drawing all of her golden parts into itself, but even her dry skin looks somehow cleaner to Sky, clearer. The creases lengthening around her widened hips are lined with dirt, but the skinny muscles in her limbs look plumper, and her lips, usually pulled tight across her brown teeth, have grown softer. He feels Tie's frustration bristle when her weight restricts her movements, when the quiet in the cave swells, but Sky believes the word Beautiful must look like a circle when it is stamped in clay, a figure curved and round.

When they reach the top of the tunnel, Tie leans her head into his to duck the low-hanging rock, and the walls expand into a shallow chamber with passageways threading off in two directions. The passage to the left is a stripe of solid black, a narrow crack that leads into the deepest, coolest cave—where Tie and Green used to sleep together but where they all sleep now. Straight ahead, chipped cement stairs rise upward to the main passageway lit purple with the coming nighttime, and the wind tunnel doubles as a draw for Mark's small cooking fire. The chamber is still clouded with smoke and Sky hears words bouncing against the cracked ceiling of the cave before he sees the speakers.

All you know are difficult stories anyway, says Mark.

As Sky approaches the fire, he recognizes Mark's hunched back and the pair of short metal pokers in his hands. The pokers drag a knot of roots away from the red coals, the twisted nubs roasted dark and sticky, and nearby Teller rests flat on the ground, cleaning his teeth idly with a fleck of wood. Although the wound on Teller's foot has sucked into a lumped scar, his injured leg still twitches, his calf springing, thigh muscles flexed all the way to his groin. His toes curl and uncurl as his shoulders tighten against his neck, turning his face to the shadows.

Teller drops his wood pick and whispers something that jolts into coughs, jerking his knees into the air, his throat muscles fighting to swallow.

How can a story possibly save you now? says Mark, but when Tie stumbles her weight forward, Mark looks up from the smoking roots. He drops his tools quickly, reaching toward her.

Sky knows how, snarls Tie. You don't have to help me do everything.

Be careful, Mark warns Sky.

Careful. Sky mouths the words silently. Care. Full.

With Tie's fingers gripping his shoulders and both of his hands holding her elbows, Sky locks his knees and Tie lowers herself near the fire. Sky smiles at Mark when Tie safely meets the ground, and for a quick breath Sky thinks Mark's clouded eyes are looking at him, his face easy and pleased, and Sky thinks this is brightness, happiness—I have been forgiven at last.

But then Sky realizes Mark is really looking at Tie, his foggy pupils filled with a big, wanting look. With his face pointed slightly into the cave, Mark can watch her tuck her curved legs to one side without looking directly at her.

I found a big root for you and Baby, Mark says to Tie.

Tie doesn't respond. Her cupped hand stretches out to Teller's sweaty forehead, and though Teller's whole body flinches under her touch, her face is soft and sad.

Teller, she says.

Only his name, the one word whispered, but it threads Sky's heart. Teller's name has become such a broken word, the opposite of whole and Rich.

Tie presses her palm over Teller's cheek, and then slips her fingers around his gripped fist.

Mark glares at their hands.

Stop it, says Mark.

Tie frowns. She shifts away from the fire, her glowing belly shrinking into the dark, but she does not let go of Teller's fingers.

Stop touching him, says Mark. Don't you understand? He can't even eat anymore.

Sky retreats into the blackness of the tunnels, but Mark's words hunt him. They claw through his fingers clapped over his ears. They hang in the open, in plain sight of Teller.

There will be more food and water when he's gone, says Mark.

The words rub and bite.

You know all of Green's stories anyway, says Mark.

Shut your mouth, Tie hisses.

I'm only saying what you already know.

Be quiet, shouts Tie.

A long silence. The burning firewood ticks into the

nerve-tensed air of the cave. When Sky finally peeks toward the fire and crawls back to the others, he can see Teller's eyes are open and rippling like water. In the low firelight, Teller's flushed cheeks are moving squares of shadow, the hollows sharpening his long nose. With the corners of his mouth stretched into his cheeks, into a tight grimace, his face is light and shadow at the same time—no color, no words. Sky shivers. It is a relief when Teller speaks. His voice is still strong even through his tight teeth.

Listen, says Teller.

Teller examines his own fingers held up before his face, trembling sticks of flesh and bone, and then looks over at Tie's stomach, at her flattened navel and her taut belly skin.

Mark and Sky, says Teller, promise me you'll help Tie. You have to remember everything when it's time.

Mark stabs at the wrinkled roots, piling their supplies.

I'll help Tie myself, says Mark. Sky kills mothers.

What's wrong with you? shouts Tie.

Inferno. The awful word burns in Sky's shivering mouth. Inferno and Waste.

No, Sky, don't cry, says Tie. It's not Baby's fault if I die.

You're not going to die, say Teller and Mark at once.

Red cramps behind Sky's eyes and his fingers smear wet around his face, trying to push the words Save Us out of his mind. The words are not big enough for the hurt and fear and worry. They are useless words, as empty as air.

What if there's blood? Sky says into his palms.

Not all the blood will be bad, says Teller to Tie. Not all blood lets in poison.

I'll make sure there's still food and firewood by then, says Mark. I'll make our fires less often.

Mark pulls the unburned end of a floorboard from his fire and the smoke swirls thick. The firelight dims on Sky's chest. The darkness in the cave grows, the shadows filling with dangerous memories.

When Tie whispers, her eyes are like holes poked in sand.

What if it's like Song and Little One? she says.

Song, murmurs Sky's old misery. He was so young he only remembers Mark keeping him outside the caves, the tunnels echoing with screams.

You're stronger than Song was, says Teller to Tie. Baby will be stronger than Little One. I know babies mean less food and water for everyone, but remember the mother story. Mothers are very special.

We'll have extra food and water, mumbles Mark at Teller, if you give up your share.

The wash water has to be boiled for a long time, says Teller with his eyes closed.

Sky, are you all right?

Everything needs to be clean when it's time.

Sky's scared.

And Baby should cry right afterwards, do you understand?

Teller, I'm scared too. Let's talk about something else.

Tie, this is important.

Let's have another story.

Listen.

Not the mother story. The story of three kings?

Tie.

Or the Enemy Ocean story?

I won't be here to help.

Tie pulls Sky against her body and presses her head into his. Though her grip pinches, her knotted hair is thick and warm. There is a soft knock from inside her stomach, a small beat against Sky's shaking chest.

Baby likes you, says Tie into the top of Sky's head. I hope when Baby comes she's just like you, quiet and helpful.

Teller closes his mouth and Mark looks at the metal tools in his hands. With one of the pokers, Mark begins stabbing the burnt stubs of firewood into bits of kindling—quick, angry chopping. The silence glares and Sky wishes Tie would stop petting him. There are cracks in the stone floor, sharp lines and shapes. Some of the cracks are wide enough to fit Sky's entire hand, but none of the cracks are wide enough to hide his whole body.

She? asks Teller at last.

I hope Baby's a girl, says Tie. We have enough boys already.

Mark nods at the splintered wood chips.

Can you tell a story now? Tie asks Teller. Please, nothing with mothers. I miss Green, I still miss him all the time. Can we hear one of his stories?

Teller closes his eyes again, and Sky stiffens his crying mouth. Don't be a baby, Mark will tell him, don't be a child. But even Mark's eyes start to leak, to admit, filling up the missing places of Green, Song, Mother, overflowing with Missing, and when Mark slams down the metal poker and leaves the fire quickly, Sky tries to call after him with a missing voice. Mark disappears into the blackness of the caves as the words cluster in Sky's throat—Mark, Brother—but the emptiness grows faster. The tunnels are dark and smothering. Sky's words come out tangled.

What did you say, Sky? asks Tie.

He said Mark, says Teller.

I think he said Mother, says Tie. Don't listen to Mark, Sky. Mark's awful.

Tie, says Teller, you have to work together.

I hate everything he says, says Tie.

You have to try harder.

No.

You have to learn. Sky too.

The firelight sinks to orange, moving shadows into their naked laps and bowed faces. As the moments pass, the nighttime blackness slowly takes the stack of sticky roots, the small pile of kindling, and it presses cool against the back of Sky's neck, ready to gulp words and names into emptiness, into the Missing, all around them the Dark Sickness closing in.

Teller's eyes revolve from the thickening gloom to Sky.

Sky, says Teller. Do you remember the Enemy Ocean story?

Sky nods at Teller.

Tell us how the story starts.

Sky's mind is suddenly zero. He shakes his head.

You remember. The story starts with the Nations of the World.

Sky nods quickly.

What happens next?

They decide to fight.

They decide to go to war, corrects Teller. War means people fighting and dying.

Like us? asks Sky.

Teller and Tie look at each other.

Sometimes, says Teller cautiously. But we make peace too, so we can help each other grow food and collect water and feel happy.

Peace, thinks Sky. Like being included. Forgiven.

Wars also have armies, says Mark's bodiless voice.

Flash pain. Sky sees white sparks after Tie's elbow surprises into the side of his head.

Sky, are you all right? asks Tie. Mark, we didn't know you were there.

Mark crawls back from the darkness and up to the fire, his feet sliding over soundless rocks. With his head tucked low, his hair almost covers his red, swollen eyes. His voice is low and upset, Sky doesn't know how much Mark overheard, but Sky is grateful to have Mark near again.

Wars have allies and enemies, says Mark.

The dim fire waves orange and brown, bringing the nighttime closer. Teller's face is already hidden in the dark, but Sky knows his eyes are saying things to Tie.

Tie lowers her head. Although she speaks into her chest, her words reach out. They sound like Peace.

Mark, do you know what comes next in the story? Tie asks.

Mark's eyes remain low, examining the large, twisted root he turns in his hands.

The flood, says Mark. The Nations called for teeth and blood to stop the Enemy Ocean from advancing. Green said when the world's soldiers came together they created an army so large their marching shook the ground flat.

And when all the soldiers spoke together, they roared like a storm, says Tie.

Mark nods down at the large root in his hands and without looking up, hands it whole to Tie. With a short claw of broken glass, he halves another smaller root, brings the first half to his open lips, puts the other half on the ground near Sky. No one speaks when Teller's portion is stored in a jar. No eyes lift from the dying firelight. The root will feel dangerous until Mark starts chewing, Sky knows, this root grown by Mark, cooked by Mark, still belonging to Mark.

The cave's blackness spreads over Teller's chest and legs. Only his cracked hand, resting empty and without food at his side, is lit orange and brown.

Sky, says Teller, his voice jumping mouthless from the dark. Who did the army fight?

The smoky root mush is less dry, the taste less bitter and starchy, if Sky lets small bites soften in his mouth before chewing. The root also lasts longer this way.

The Enemy Ocean, says Sky finally.

Why?

Don't know.

You do, says Teller. You have to remember everything, Sky.

Because, says Sky and then with a bigger voice, because the Enemy Ocean turned to poison. Then it sank the islands and it began to take the land.

And?

And homes.

From who?

People.

The progeny, interrupts Mark. They were from different places and looked different from each other and told different stories. Some ate roots like us, but others ate wheat or rice or the flesh of creatures. They all hated each other before the war, but they became allies when the Enemy Ocean awoke.

Mark glances at Tie and at the same moment Sky's memory flickers, a splash to the first time he swam in the ocean, the heat of the brown waves, the floating, gritty plastic. Green's beard moves as he warns Sky not to put his face under the seawater, his supporting arms dropping away, leaving Sky to kick and paddle on his own for the first time.

Promise to stay near the beach, Green said. There's no swimming away from here.

Sorrow quickly blankets the bright details of the memory, a grayness brought on simply in the remembering, the past changing itself, altering the meaning of Green's words, but still, beyond and beneath the painful missing, Sky does not recall any fear of the ocean, no pressing, no piercing terror. Sometimes, thinks Sky, untrue things happen in stories.

Teller nods at Mark.

There were also different kinds of soldiers in the army, says Teller.

As he speaks, Teller takes deep breaths. His hand spasms make his fingers grip and release, grip and release. The firelight colors his knuckles orange then brown, orange then brown.

There were soldiers from all parts of the world, says Teller. Some were stronger than others so they were given important tasks, like caring for everyone's food and water. Some of them had to work all day and night, and some had scars on their faces, signs of their bravery from past wars.

One of Mark's hands moves halfway to the scar on his nose, then drops quickly back to his root.

It was only a rock, mutters Mark, referring to the chunk that fell from the cave ceiling and created the scar that would name him, but Sky can tell Mark is pleased.

There were also soldiers with wisdom, says Teller, his hand moving slightly toward Tie. They knew the firewood story, the mother story, the story of three kings, all the stories about wars, and not just the wars that were won, because it's important to remember mistakes too, so they won't be repeated and the dead won't be forgotten.

Tie bows her frown, her finger tracing a jagged crack in the ground.

And there were young soldiers in the army, says Teller. They were strong and brave even as the Enemy Ocean rose, after Moth flew into the sky. With all the progeny cooperating and working together, the army was powerful, not just because it was large but because it had many brave, smart, and different people in it.

But it was too late, right? asks Sky.

The small circle of fire breathes red and brown, and a black dot grows in the heart of the coals. Sky can feel the air in the cave changing, swirling around the word Peace, around Wisdom, around all of them sitting close and together, and he is excited, excited to be a part of the story, to be included, with everyone finally patient with each other, Forever—I want everyone to be helping each other and safe and happy forever.

But when Teller speaks, his voice is Careful. Care. Full.

Yes, Teller says to Sky, but there's more to the story than that. What's important is that everyone worked together.

That's not only what's important, says Tie.

In the near darkness, Sky can see Tie's head lift, her

hand falling from the tall shelf of her belly. When she speaks, her words are empty tins.

Sky's right, says Tie. It was too late for the Nations to win.

We can change that part of the story, says Mark, glaring at Sky. We can give the story any ending we want. It doesn't matter.

Yes it does, says Tie, her voice starting to boil. We already left out the parts when the Enemy Ocean turns to radiant blood and all the sea monsters wash up on the beaches. We're already forgetting those parts of the story, Green's story, and now we're going to forget the ending too? The story always ends this way, when Green told it and when Song told it before him.

Teller lifts his hand to say Stop.

That's how the story goes, she says to Mark. That's how the story ends.

A story is made of many parts, says Teller. The ending isn't the only important part.

Yes it is, shouts Tie. Is this all we do? Remember only the happy parts of stories, of Green—

It doesn't matter, interrupts Mark loudly, his flat hand chopping downward. Just because you miss him doesn't mean I'm awful.

So Mark heard Tie from the shadows, hating him, hating his words while he was in earshot. Sky ducks his guilty head but Tie charges her voice at Teller.

Mistakes, she shouts. You want to remember mistakes?

How about Green's mistakes? I have to be special but he gets to decide how he dies?

Tie, what do you mean? whispers Teller.

Tie's outrage flares open, sucking the air from Sky's lungs.

You know what I mean, she yells. You all know what I mean.

Tie, says Teller.

The Nations tried to stop the Enemy Ocean—

Please—

—and they failed, they died and they failed—

The coals in the fire blacken, sink to smoke, but Tie's cries continue in the tunnels, her fists lunging at shadowy, unspoken ghosts. Mark darts away again, and this time Sky hears the clank of the metal buckets in the main passageway—Mark going to the beach for wash water. It is still scalding outside, the evening too hot and energy-sucking to leave the cave, but Sky scrambles after Mark with Tie's angry voice leaping against the cave walls.

I don't want a baby, I don't want to be special—

Tie's words multiply and overlap in the tunnels.

I want Green, I want things like before—

The massive space outside the cave meets Sky's skin like a burst of fiery breath. The open night still burns with the daytime storms, and it thickens Sky's skin to rubber as he listens to the sound of Tie's yells, her screams—Song's screams. He hops eagerly away from Tie's snapping words and after Mark, blistering the soles of his feet on the cooked ground and sweating precious water as he climbs down the dunes. With the growing sound of the sea, the increasing smell of ocean rot, there is also a distant, rising glow at the shoreline.

And then brightness, brilliance—an enormous rolling blue. At the beach, the waves crash into color, spreading a pebbled and heat-rippled light across the sands. The glimmering fades, it smashes bright again, constant movement, the entire coastline breathing and glowing blue. Radiant, Sky whispers to himself, Radiant. The breakers shimmer around the dark shape of Mark, two buckets hanging from his hands, but when Sky runs up to help him collect the wash water, Mark throws an arm out.

Stay away from the water, says Mark. Red tide.

But it's blue, says Sky, though he doesn't remember Green ever mentioning a blue tide.

The color doesn't matter, says Mark. It's all poison.

Like the Enemy Ocean? asks Sky, but Mark turns quickly, his knuckles slamming the air from Sky's stomach.

It's just a story, shouts Mark with his fists still clenched. Do you hear me? Just a story. None of it is true.

Sky sinks down to the scorching sand, holds his knees against his knotted belly as Mark trudges back to the cave with the empty buckets. Sometimes, Sky scolds himself, untrue things happen in stories. He repeats this to himself while he watches the light and dark colors pulse along the beach, tells himself Radiant as the waves roll blue and toxic, but the word he feels is Lonely under the pressing, piercing night.

CHAPTER FOUR

Sky crouches in the deep and crowding dark. Blinking does not change the cave's blackness. Days of sleep have not weakened it. The small, painful lights no longer appear when he rubs his knuckles into his closed eyelids, so he grips the split floor of the cave. His fingers and toes dig into cracks worn smooth by bare feet, into the damp stones that suck warmth. At least he remembers their names. Hard. Slippery. There are broken rocks as well. Sharp. Dangerous. He thought he knew the words for darkness too, but without light all talk has shrunk quiet. After so long in the lowest sleeping chamber, waiting out the storms and the choking heat of deep summer, it is not the usual dark of sleep or tunnel crawling. In the stillness, closed in by the smells of stale smoke and sour bodies, the blackness has grown. It pours into Sky's open eyes, widens inside of his ears. What used to be shallow, dormant breathing is now one large noise bouncing off the cave walls, and under the weight of the underground darkness, he cannot tell where the others are anymore. He cannot reach to them and he cannot bring himself to speak to them. In the shadows, his loudest words are his oldest. Thirsty. Hungry. Afraid. These words will not end the Dark Sickness.

The pressure increases as noise grows in the tunnel, in the cave above. There is a dreamy shout from the main passageway that might be real, distant footsteps and wood planks dragging over loose gravel. Scrap. No, the word is Scrape—scraping. When Sky unwraps his arms from around his narrow chest, the air in the cave swirls against his skin. Now he knows there will be fire and light. There will be shapes and figures and words pulled out of shadow, out of emptiness. His mouth waters. Footsteps draw closer and the dragging stops. Sky remains still, breathing and waiting.

There is a thin scratching, the sound of wood scrubbing. The noise quickens. Sky licks his lips when he tastes the bitter smoke. A distant light opens—a swelling red in the cave above—and when Mark's stick of lit firewood bobs around the curve in the tunnel, Sky has to shield his eyes against the thudding brightness.

Come look, says Mark. I found something.

The sleeping breath around him breaks. A listening quiet.

Come see, says Mark, and the stabbing light retreats to the upper cave.

Waking movements in the shadows. Sky drifts his hands into the dark and touches the cool skin of Tie's back. She has already lifted herself onto her hands and knees, but when he tries to help her stand, she throws his arm away. Clutching the wall of the tunnel, she climbs out of the sleeping chamber on her own, so Sky stretches his fingers into the blackness to find Teller. He feels the burning in the air before he feels Teller's hot and sticky face, his shaking limbs. Teller has managed to turn himself onto his side, but it is Sky who rolls him onto his stomach so he can crawl.

Ready? whispers Sky when Teller has lifted himself. One, two, three.

With his arms wrapped around Teller's middle, Sky heaves him a step forward. Teller groans, readjusts his arms and knees under his body, and Sky heaves again. Though Sky was to conserve his energy with sleep, to slow his heartbeat and tighten his breath into a small, hungerless lump in his stomach, he is quickly exhausted, his parched throat sucking hoarse. He rests frequently, listening to Teller gasp, and by the time they reach the cave above, Mark's low fire is already too hot to sit near. There are pots of drinking water and wash water resting in the coals, as well as carefully cropped roots warming, a collection of clean water jars ready to be filled, a small heap of sandy wood chips—all Mark's work. The smoke drags upward into the main passageway, which is nighttime dark, and Mark and Tie rest at the cooler end of the cave, their heads bowed to a shape between them, a large and orb-like object.

Sky manages to heave Teller one last time before Teller collapses flat onto his side, bloodless and panting. He drags hissing air through his clamped jaw, but even as his muscles gather into knots and contract his knees into the air, sound pushes through his gritted teeth.

Water, hisses Teller.

Mark looks up from the round object, his sun-blistered forehead crossed over flared and sleepless eyes.

I just started the water, how many hands do you think I have? says Mark. If I have to do everything while everyone else does nothing, then you're going to have to wait.

The word Nothing rings through Sky's bones, stinging the cores of his eyes, the stem of his voiceless tongue. Days and nights in the suffocating sleeping chamber, saturated in a pooling bodily stench as the other two slept, his mind growing wordless but always quicker, always nervous, in that scream of dangerous memories, that deep underground quiet, a silence broken only by Teller's groans and spasms and yelps. Dripping water into Teller's mouth as his teeth snapped, forced to wash Tie where she could not reach, wiping them both low and between their legs like the others used to bathe him as a child. Like babies, he kept telling his inept and frightened hands, bathe them like children.

But Nothing, Nothing, Mark thinks I am Nothing. He told me to stay with Tie and Teller, he told me to keep them fed and washed and empty their buckets while Mark looked for firewood and took care of the food and water, and I only tried to please you, you, my brother, but I am Nothing in the dark, Nothing in Nothingness.

Sky's face burns and when he stands to rush away, his knees wobble. The effort to move Teller drops Sky's blood into his feet, flattening his drained body against the floor of the cave. His throat grates as air pulls deep into his chest—one breath, two, three—and gradually his vision becomes steadier, his thoughts more clear.

The Dark Sickness eases.

Slowly, Sky's heartbeat calms as the shifting firelight pulls the others out of the greasy dark—orange noses and foreheads, mouths smeared with grime. The scar across Mark's nose has a moving shadow of its own, a ghost hiding in the grooved line between his crooked eyebrows, his hazy eyes. Brother. Powerful. Besides his bubbled sunburns and the new, dark wisps on his breastbone, Mark has changed the least since the last fire. Tie's square face, framed by all her long, brown knots of hair, is now much sharper, her slender shoulders narrower, than her large, ripe stomach that rests wide in her lap. The rippling firelight makes her belly look like a water drop about to fall from a fingertip, like a smooth stone Sky wants to roll in his hands, but the light also shows the deep gaps between Teller's shuddering ribs. Teller's clenched jaw makes strings of his cheek and neck muscles, and the hair on his upper lip shines with sweat. Should not, should not have slipped and let met- al poison climb up the cut in his foot, Sky tells himself. He has commanded the thought into his mind for many nights, bracing himself in the blackness. At least Teller has already outlived Song, thinks Sky, and just as Song's empty body was dragged outside the cave, soon so will Teller's.

If Mark and Tie can feel the looming Dark Sickness, Sky cannot tell. They both stare at the round object between them while Tie massages the small of her back with her knuckles, as Mark unties the plastic ropes from around his scabbed and burned feet, the cords sandy and melted from the heat of the sun-cooked beach.

It was floating in the tide pools, says Mark. Maybe it can be useful.

He prods at the orb, larger than a human head, and Sky lifts himself to sitting as the globe rocks heavy and hollow. It sways with a small clicking sound inside of it, like rolling pebbles. There is a smooth shell of white paint underneath the skin of brown ocean decay. The white is pocked by brown rot where seawater weathered the paint, but when Sky moves closer he can see carved indents in the treated wood, raised shapes and etched decorations, swirls on one half, sharper twists on the other, two matching circles on the top and bottom.

What is it? Tie asks.

Teller's red-rimmed eyes peel open.

It's wood at least, says Mark. Maybe it's a tool, or part of one.

I don't think so, says Tie. It has two eyes.

Teller tilts his sweaty face toward the object. He inhales.

A creature, whispers Teller.

Mark straightens back from the object.

Creatures are only in stories, says Mark.

Maybe a jumping creature, asks Tie, like in the fire-wood story?

Even if it is, says Mark, then it's a dead creature and it's useless.

Tie picks up the globe and turns it gently around in her hands. Its insides clink and rattle. When Tie speaks, her voice is vague, listening and remembering.

Mother used to tap shingles together and call them her toys, says Tie. She said the sound scared away the nightmares.

The Dark Sickness, says Sky, surprised by his own rasping voice.

Tie looks at him, her eyes strangely distant.

That's right, she says quietly. Green called it Dark Sickness.

Sky winces. It has been many quiet nights since Tie's screaming, since the last time Green's name was spoken.

That's why, chokes Teller, his neck threads standing. That's why Green told so many stories in the summer.

We haven't been telling stories and we're fine, says Mark annoyed. We don't need stories.

Tie shakes the globe so suddenly and viciously that Sky and Mark's shoulders jump and Teller's body flexes into an arch. The cave vibrates with the loud, clattering racket, and when Tie stops rattling the noisemaker, her clenched jaw ripples the muscles of her cheeks.

We aren't fine, says Tie, and the globe makes a final clank when she drops it to the ground.

Mark crawls across the cave, as close to the fire as he can bear, and with one hand held up against his face and his other hand wrapped with plastic cords, he uses the short metal poker to lift the boiling water pots out of the coals.

When Tie speaks again, her voice cracks high and sad, addressing no one.

Green was a part of every task and every conversation, says Tie. And now every memory of him hurts.

As her shoulders wilt into her body and Teller's muscles slowly release their grip, Mark moves back to Tie's side, placing a clay bowl of steaming water beside her. With his hand near her knee, Mark's fogged pupils shine bright with firelight.

You're a part of every task too, he says to Tie. You know how to tie the strongest cords and you're the best at fixing the fog net. We wouldn't have this water if it weren't for you.

Tie tilts her head, studying the clay bowl.

And you're a part of all our conversations, Mark says. You always see two sides of an argument.

Teller hacks, clearing his tight throat.

You also know two sides of Green, says Teller. You know all his stories.

The fire wrinkles shadows across the walls of the cave. Mark's hand moves to Tie's knee.

You're holding on too hard, says Mark to Tie. I think

if you started to forget Green, you might see your part in everything.

Teller shakes his head slightly as Mark continues.

Maybe if you let some memories go, there will be room for new memories.

Can never forget our past, says Teller.

That doesn't mean Tie should torture herself, snaps Mark. I would have tortured myself thinking about Mother, if I hadn't turned my mind to my work.

Ignoring the past, says Teller, doesn't make it go away.

Lies don't help either—

Stories are sacred.

Need to move forward—

—to honor and reflect—

Stop, says Tie, her hands raised. Let me think.

Teller and Mark sit quietly, unblinking, and Sky watches Tie press her forehead into her palms, her eyes closed and lips moving without sound. When she opens her eyes, she is looking at the decayed globe again.

What if this thing means the stories are true? she asks.

Teller gazes at the silent globe.

What if, says Teller, and he sucks in a long breath. What if it's a message from Moth?

Teller's sick eyes widen, black and shining, staring hard at the globe.

Mark snorts a cold laugh.

Well, says Mark, I guess our problems are over. Maybe

I'll get some sleep, since we don't have to worry about food or water anymore.

Teller closes his eyes and twitching lips. He swallows with a gulp.

This is more important than food or water—the stories have always been more important, says Teller. This means Moth might be speaking to us.

What are you talking about, says Mark with no asking in his voice.

Like the story of Moon and Bear, or the story of three kings.

Fever, says Mark low to Tie.

They'll come and rescue us, shouts Teller.

Rescue, thinks Sky, a word so old it has rotten hollow. Older than Hungry or Thirsty. More helpless than Afraid.

Teller, says Tie with worry lines along her forehead. Teller, drink some water.

Tie hands the steaming water bowl to Sky, but as he tries to dribble water over Teller's clamped teeth, Teller turns his face toward the ground, his lips stirring quietly. Sky shifts his ear closer to hear words pant and click from Teller's moving tongue, low and repeating.

When the Great Fires began and Moth flew into the sky—

Teller's words are pressed so tightly together they sigh, a long prayer called back from so many fiery days ago when Teller spoke over Green's body.

Determination and hope, determination and hope—

Mark glares, his chin souring.

So now he doesn't want any water, says Mark as Sky returns the bowl.

Teller, we don't know what this thing is, says Tie looking at the strange globe. We know Moth flies away in the story of three kings—

Teller, with his lips still turning and eyes staring, nods.

Maybe it would help to hear the story again. We don't have to sing it like Song or—Tie pauses—or remember all of Green's words. We can tell the story any way we want.

Tie looks at the globe, at the Moth message, and then at Mark.

We will remember and make new memories at the same time, she says.

Tie sucks the steam from the water bowl through her nose, swirls a mouthful to rinse her teeth clean, and swallows the liquid down.

When Mark has refilled the bowl and finished his portion, Sky is handed the bowl with the remaining liquid. The surface of the water trembles as his shaking hands bring the bowl to his lips, the fluid drenches his sticky tongue, and watery heat expands along the cord of his throat. Sweet. The one word fills Sky's mind and explodes. Sweet.

When we were young, says Tie to Mark, the story of three kings was your favorite.

I didn't know anything then, mutters Mark. Anyway, I mostly liked the counting game.

Can you tell the story?

Mark scoffs, pitching a bit of gravel toward the fire, but shies when he sees Tie's intent face, her asking eyes. After a moment, he shrugs a shy shoulder. He holds up his pointer finger to count One.

The story of three kings, says Mark, begins when the Enemy Ocean awoke—

Before Moth flew into the sky, whispers Teller.

—before Moth flew into the sky, mumbles Mark. There were three kings who hated each other. The first king liked fighting—

Mark glances down at Teller. Teller is watching and whispering, and Mark shakes his head, drops his hand.

I don't know all of Teller's words, says Mark.

The story is told in patterns of three, that's how the counting game works, says Tie. Just count what you remember.

What I remember, repeats Mark, and extends again a single finger.

The first three fingers are for the kings, says Mark, squinting at his pointer finger. One is for the first king, who had the strongest army in the world. Outside his city people were always fighting and inside people were always being punished, but the first king only had to give his word and all the scared people would follow him.

What was the word? asks Sky, the question leaping from his mouth.

Mark rolls his eyes and holds up another finger to count Two.

Two is for the second king, who had the most food and water in the world. Outside his city people were always starving and inside people were always greedy and wasting, but the second king only had to promise riches and all the desperate people would follow him.

And Three, says Mark with three fingers raised, is for the third king, who was elected by his people and who had the largest city in the world. Outside his city people wanted things done one way and inside people wanted things done another way. The third king had enough people to defeat any army in the world, but it could take years for everyone to cooperate.

Mark frowns at his three fingers.

The killing comes next? he asks.

The gifts, whispers Teller from the ground and Tie nods.

Right, the next three fingers, says Mark remembering. The Nations of the World needed the kings to make peace, so three messengers were sent with gifts of gold, perfume, and oil.

Mark raises another finger to count Four.

When the messenger reached the first city, says Mark, the first king cut off the messenger's head. He stole the gift of gold and named himself the strongest king in the world.

Mark extends his thumb, his open hand showing Five.

When the messenger reached the second city, the second king burned the messenger alive. He stole the gift of perfume and as the smell rose into the sky, he named himself a god.

Mark holds up a finger on his free hand, making the number Six.

And when the last messenger reached the third city, the third king didn't accept or reject the gift of oil, so his people named the third king a traitor and called for his death.

Sky's stomach growls loudly at the word Oil, groaning with the thought of greasy root skins and pulpy plant flesh. As he crosses his arms tightly across his belly to silence it, Sky hears another groan from Tie's direction and he nearly laughs at Tie's stomach answering his own.

But when he looks into Tie's face her mouth is twisted into a pained snarl, her brown teeth bared and eyes pinched shut. Like Sky, her arms are held tightly across her stomach, but her fingers search the huge surface of her stretched belly skin, pressing low, around, and under her navel.

Are you all right? asks Mark with Six still raised in the air.

Teller's eyes are also on Tie.

There's, says Tie, with her lips curled. There's water.

You want water? asks Mark reaching toward the fire. There is still Teller's portion.

But when Mark brings the steaming bowl to Tie, she bows her head and lowers herself onto her side, breasts slumping against the cave floor. A strange damp smell, watery sweet, fills Sky's nose.

I need, she whispers, to lie still.

With Tie's eyes squeezed closed and her fingers netted around her bulged stomach, Sky feels the uselessness of his hands, his empty palms. The only thing he can think to do is lift Tie's head into his lap to ease her angled neck as Mark places the water bowl within Tie's reach.

Teller watches Mark settle the water bowl as well, the bowl pinned under his thirsty stare. Tie continues to hug her belly, her face colorless.

Say something, moans Tie with her eyes shut. Something.

For an instant, Sky and Mark's eyes meet, worry finding worry.

Something, repeats Mark. Yes, the story.

Mark clears his throat, leaping six fingers into the air again.

So only the third messenger returned and empty-handed, he says quickly. The Nations of the World could not make—I mean, could not form—and the world was like a knot tightening, like a muscle that becomes more tense as it bleeds—

Mark stops with his hands held up, and Tie's eyelids flick open. Those are Green's words, thinks Sky, knowing everyone is thinking the same.

The fire sparks against the cave walls and the wind in the passageway moves through their group silence. When Tie finally speaks, her voice is steady.

That's why the progeny rose up.

Mark dips his head, his eyes darting sideways at Tie, then at the roots glistening near the fire.

This is the part where someone else counts, mutters Mark.

Want to count first, Tie asks Sky with an exhale, touching his ankles with sticky fingertips, but Teller raises a shaking hand from the ground, his boney fingers tucked into a loose fist. His dark eyes roll away from the water bowl and fix on Mark. Determination and hope, thinks Sky.

As Mark continues the story, Teller's mouth pulls into a strained grin.

The next three fingers are for the progeny, says Mark. Outside the first city, where everyone was always fighting, the progeny convinced the people to throw rocks at the soldiers, driving them away.

So it was said the progeny could move stones without touching them.

Teller extends a single finger, counting One.

Inside the first city, continues Mark, the progeny opened the prisons, bringing people out of darkness. So it was said the progeny—

—could make blind men see, says Teller as he lifts a second finger, signaling Mark to go on.

And when the progeny reached the first king, grumbles Mark, who wore a crown made of the stolen gold, they called out the name of the first man, waking first life.

Atom, said the progeny. Fuse.

And the gold answered the call, says Mark. The gold grew so hot on top of the king's head that it melted over his face and shoulders and the first king was roasted to death.

Teller lifts a final finger to count Three, and then lowers his arm onto the floor of the cave, smiling his gapped teeth. He turns his large eyes to the wooden globe near his face, examining the detailed lines. Mark raises a seventh finger as Tie's body tightens.

It's too hot here, gasps Tie in Sky's lap. Sweat stands on her furrowed forehead as she pants.

Too hot, she repeats, her palms searching the ground for cool stones.

The roots aren't done, says Mark shaking his head. We can't put out the fire yet.

Tie's fingers crawl across the ground in front of her, blindly reaching closer to the water bowl. Teller's stare widens when her nails scratch the clay lip, as water trickles over the dish's edge. The bowl upends the same moment Mark shouts Stop and the word No pushes out of Teller's teeth, and Sky can only watch the handful of water cross the cave floor, his mouth drying as the trickle escapes from Teller drilling gaze and gathers against Tie's body.

Hot, says Tie quieter, her eyes closed tight. What's happening?

It's gone, says Mark, watching the water sink between the stones. When he speaks to Sky, Mark's voice is dangerously slow, his eyes burned open.

We need to move her into the lower cave, says Mark. Pick up her legs. Don't lift too high.

Sky jumps up to wrap his arms around Tie's knees, where the damp smell is the strongest. He thought the drinking water spilled against her stomach, but her legs are slippery too. He thought there was just a swallow of water in the bowl, but there's water between Tie's thighs as well.

Let me do it, Tie growls as they rotate her onto her back, her hip bones popping, and when Mark lifts Tie into a sitting position, she yelps at such a high pitch that Sky freezes in place. Tie's brown eyes are open, staring at nothing, her lips sucking air quickly. Teller, who has been whispering again to the globe, tears his eyes away from the spilled water, ejecting words in exhales.

Tie, breathes Teller.

We'll lift her carefully, a little bit at a time, says Mark to Sky.

Clean, breathes Teller. Water.

We'll start by getting her to the tunnel, says Mark.

Baby, breathes Teller.

Lift on three. One, two—

Mark.

Be quiet, Teller—

Sky.

Clean water for Baby, answers Sky. I remember, Teller. Don't worry.

—one, two, three.

CHAPTER FIVE

Stop, groans Tie.

Sky and Mark lower Tie gently to the slanted floor of the tunnel. In the slim and jagged passageway, halfway into the pitch dark of the sleeping chamber, Tie, Mark, and Sky suck the smoky air. Tie's clenched body is too wide to rotate in the narrow space, so Mark has been carrying her backward through the tunnel, back-stepping in small, guarded shuffles. Their path also drops too sharply into the blackness for Tie to rest flat, so instead of laying her with her head pointed downward, Mark props her into a recline, her shoulder blades resting back against his.

In this position, Mark can support all of Tie's weight and Sky is relieved. There is only sound, scent, and touch in the tunnel's darkness, and Tie's new smell is worrying, her rapid breaths make his chest thump acid, make his muscles braid. When it is safe to release Tie's legs, Sky scrambles away, forcing his breath to slow while wiping sweat from his grainy eyes. The fast stabbing in his ribs lessens as he pulls air deeply through his nose, and his shivering body calms when he releases air slowly through his mouth.

As his blood begins to steady, he hears Tie matching his breath. He reaches out to her knees again and feels her body slowly loosening its grip.

It's a little better, says Tie after a long inhale and a long exhale.

I can't stay here, says Mark. The roots will burn, the drinking water needs to be jarred, then the fire—

I'll check the roots, says Sky, and he trots up the passage before Mark can stop him. Above, in the red firelight of the upper cave, the heat has grown to wringing, and Sky notices at once that Teller has moved. He has dragged himself closer to the fire, his ribs pumping fast from the effort. The hot touch of his skin stings Sky's fingertips, but he still tugs Teller away from the fire, to where the warmth is drawn upward into the windy main passageway already lit gray with early morning.

You're going to hurt yourself, says Sky to Teller.

Teller, heat-knocked and staring, does not answer.

Try to rest, says Sky.

Back at the fire, the skins of the roots have already shriveled black on one side, so Sky quickly retrieves the metal pokers to remove the nubs from the heat. The dying fire burns his face and the metal bites his fingers, but he manages to arrange the cooling roots in such a way that they do not touch, the same way Mark arranges them, then uses the pokers to spread and thin the gleaming coals. The black chunks he brushes into the charcoal heap, near the snapped blades and dull claws of glass, and he nudges the pot of boiled wash water and rags into a dark corner. By that time, the drinking water has cooled enough to pour into the glass jars.

A cautious pause. Sky searches Teller's face—his unseeing eyes, the awful knots in his cheeks—then glances toward Mark and Tie, who are hidden from sight around the bend in the tunnel. Sky has never handled the cooking before and Mark has never trusted him with pouring the water, but even as the dread of failure folds his shoulders, he knows, at that moment, there is no one else to do the work. He begins lining up the jars the way he has seen Mark organize them before, from largest to smallest. The iron pot is heavy in both of Sky's shaking hands, but the importance of the job, the weight of the task, orders his mind and muscles to a focused point. I am not Nothing, he thinks, I am here and I am able—I will take care of the work for Mark.

The water in the pot sloshes as Sky tips the wobbling load toward the jars, and Sky forces his thin elbows to steady, to pour the water even more gradually toward the pot's spouted edge. At last, water trickles into the first jar and Sky waits for the last drop to fall before moving onto the next. Six jars he fills to their brims, then half of the seventh, all so painfully slow but without one bit spilt, just like Mark would have done himself, able and Responsible—I poured the water just like Mark.

And when Sky places the pot on the cave's stone floor with an empty clang, Teller's stare is no longer blank. Teller watches the jars as they are lidded and gathered, his eyes bright but without praise, aware but not of Sky. His lips move weakly as Sky stows the jars inside the pot.

Water, says Teller.

Sky looks at the half-empty jar, the seventh and smallest.

We already drank tonight's water, says Sky.

Teller's mouth continues to rotate, perhaps praying quietly, to his stories, to Moth, to his determination and hope.

But Sky hears the word again from Teller's mouth. Water.

Mark said—

Water.

Refuse, thinks Sky. Mark would refuse Teller without blinking, because indecisive kings are traitors. Mark would be able to deny Teller, to flatten memories of better days, of Teller well and strong, singing loud over the ocean wind as he repaired the fog net, his voice happy and clear. Refuse and work instead of allowing hope to pry open the emptiness, making room for the Dark Sickness. With his eyes on the ground, Sky feels this new, cold responsibility in the stems of his fingers, following him into the solid dark of the tunnel toward Mark and Tie.

In the oily shadows, Sky hears murmuring.

Won't let anything happen to you, says Mark.

Mark's voice—it jerks Sky to a stop. It is an odd voice, unrecognizable. A strange thought pangs through Sky's mind—Mark is afraid.

I promise I won't let anything bad happen, says Mark.

Nothing you can do, says Tie.

I can do something?

It's no use.

Tie.

Terrors cram into the stillness, crowding the childish and begging parts of Sky's mind. A sharp gloom sets in, and Sky speaks to lop the hungry silence, to fling the Dark Sickness away.

I took care of the roots, he nearly shouts into the tunnel.

More terrible wordlessness.

They're cooling now, continues Sky, and the water was cool enough to jar—

What, yells Mark, his voice flung in Sky's direction. Did you spill any? There should be six and a half jars. If you spilt any—

Didn't spill, says Sky quickly, shrinking to the ground near Tie's knees.

It's all right, says Tie. He did all right.

Mark remains quiet in the dark. When Sky shifts himself near Tie, he can tell she is breathing fast again. The skin of her legs is slick with sweat.

Teller needs water, says Sky, though he already knows this is useless talk. At least the words are not as pointless as Teller Needs Help or Save Teller.

Needs water, repeats Mark in a toxic voice, with a slow and exhausted sigh.

When he finally answers, Tie flinches as though she's been cut.

What should we do about Teller? asks Mark.

The silence returns, bearing with it a wave of Dark Sickness even heavier and more poisonous than before. Mark's are dangerous words, the ones kept low and unspoken. They make Sky's stomach twist. Cold fear rises in Sky's chest as sour rises in his throat.

What are you talking about? says Tie cautiously.

You know, says Mark.

I don't.

Fine.

A pause.

He's suffering, says Mark.

Stop, says Tie.

We have to do something.

I told you, says Tie. There's nothing you can do.

Another pause.

It's morning, says Sky with a high, unfamiliar voice. Soon it will be too hot to go to the storeroom.

No one answers. Sky pushes again, desperate for the simple talk of chores.

I can take the roots and water to the storeroom? he asks.

No, says Mark. We'll finish moving Tie and then I'll go.

No, moans Tie. Not yet.

But then—

Mark groans with frustration.

—then if Sky's going, he can't step anywhere but in the middle of the storeroom. The container's next to the last water drum, and don't forget to glass the light or dust will ruin everything, do you understand?

Yes, says Sky, and he's already on his feet. Before he disappears around the bend in the tunnel, he stops to ask, What do I say to Teller?

Tell him, begins Mark, but his answer dangles.

A breathing quiet.

Tell him to wait until sunset, says Tie at last.

As Sky creeps back into the upper chamber, he is already speaking the words.

Teller, he says, Mark and Tie say you have to wait—

But he discovers Teller has moved again. He has crawled to the cooler part of the cave, his arms locked straight in front of him but with his head and shoulders arched backwards. Teller could be stretching, just waking from a long nap, except the fading firelight shows his stringed muscles flexed near to snapping, his ribs rashed where he has pushed himself along the rough floor of the cave. Although Teller's fingers are clenched, his fists still peddle ahead, grasping at the pot with its seven jars of water.

From Teller's strained mouth, a low clicking. The sound of words trapped inside a locked jaw. A tongue speaking without sound.

Teller, tries Sky again. Mark and Tie said—

Teller isn't listening. His paled knuckles scuttle against the rough side of the pot, so Sky steps forward. He removes the pot from Teller's reach and begins piling the cooled roots on top of the lidded water jars.

So sorry, whispers Sky when Teller's clicking grows faster. Teller's arms jerk tight against his sides when the pot is moved away, his fists curled into his armpits, and Sky quickly ties plastic cords around his own bare feet so he can leave the cave faster, escape the clustered muscles of Teller's forehead, his wide and pleading eyes. Should not have let the Enemy Ocean climb up the blood in his foot, Sky repeats to himself, should not have, should not, this is not my fault, My fault, must stay strong and responsible and refuse—

Then Teller's spine flexes a loud groan from his thin chest—the sound of popping bone. Sky's steps quicken to his shrieking thoughts, his spinning, writhing guilt—Not my fault, do you hear me? Not, should not have slipped, should not, So sorry, I cannot save you, nothing I can do, Nothing—

His stomach twists so painfully he barely notices the early morning heat waving on the stairs or the rising winds slicing the main passageway. The huge, open daylight at the cave entrance blinds him through his eyelids, but soon Sky is feeling his way to the shadows of the tallest tunnel with light-splotched vision, through the slender space that leads to the storeroom.

At the last step into the damp space, Sky tries to ignore the warning ring in his mind. Go in, Mark sent me, I'm allowed to enter—remove the loose brick from the wall to create some light, put a piece of glass in the hole to block out the dust, do not step anywhere but in the middle of the room, do not move too quickly, do not be a baby.

It takes Sky's strained eyes a moment to adjust to the flash of daylight once he scratches the brick free from the wall and lodges the gap with Mark's smeared shard of glass. The rectangle of morning light, which has already grown a hotter yellow, falls directly onto the bubbled soil at the far end of the storeroom, brightening small chips of flaking mirror and the crispy white hairs of the summer roots. Slowly, though, everything else emerges as he remembers it from many days ago, the row of water drums, the iron beams supporting the ceiling—the winding lines of Forever writing. The scratched-out pattern is just as looping and intricate as when Sky first saw it, packed with silent words that lightning Sky's mind. What hides in the past beneath the quiet, he wonders. Perhaps only chore talk, but maybe secrets, answers—a place where memories are stored. Stories. The streak of daylight also leans into the square dots in the clay, the ones Mark taught him were names, that Teller said held vital stories.

Vital, Sky says aloud, and more cramping guilt tightens through him. With the heft of the pot in his arms, the weight of food and water, Vital is for supplies, Vital is for pulses, not for scratches in clay as Teller told him. With Teller's body attacking itself and Tie's wet, unsteady legs, Sky wants to hang the word Traitor, not Vital, on his name and the dots of the past.

Just remember me tomorrow, Green used to say.

The memory strikes so suddenly that grief surprises him, cracking his guilt into sorrow, filling his chest like foul water fills a jar.

Just remember me tomorrow, Green used to say whenever he took over someone else's work, when he declined portions of his food so others could eat, before he went to sleep.

Sky screws up his burning eyes and shakes his head to clear his mind. Responsibility, food and water—not these other responses. Mark once told him, You'll work better with your mouth shut, and Sky cannot help but wonder at the purpose of writing, the shadows of words after they're gone. What's talk when there's water to swallow and food to chew, and what's a past when there's work to fill the emptiness with vitals? There are memories of Green and Green crying in the storeroom, but Teller honors the dead, and food and water are my responsibility now.

To stop his thoughts of Green from surprising him again, Sky taps his fingers loudly against the sides of the water drums, discovering the first is empty, also the second, the third, the drums so awfully empty, all except for the last two at the end, both already halfway depleted. It may or may not be enough to get them through the last days of summer—the complicated tallies on the wall still mean little to Sky. Mark's count has to be correct, though, it has to be, and the best Sky can do is stow their provisions. He searches out the plastic container for the water and roots, finds the large, lidded bin near the final water drums, half-buried in the ground and hidden underneath a heap of plastic tarps. Once the container is popped he knows he will have to move fast, so no floating dust will get into their clean supplies.

But when he opens the container, Sky realizes how much he has relied on Mark. The container is entirely empty, an open, hungry mouth, and worse, he has no idea if this is normal for this time of summer. He stacks the roots quickly at one end of the container, the roots looking small and sickly, shrunken kinks of skin rather than dense plant bulbs. And once the roots are inside, the container feels even more empty. He lines the water jars at the other end of the container and decides to leave the pot inside as well, just to fill the lonely space. By the time he confirms that the container is tightly closed, he is moving quicker in the shadows, trying to get away from the empty drums and the quiet, to escape the thick responsibility of painful, vital tasks.

When Sky scratches the glass free and slides the brick back into the wall, the howling daylight he blocks out is a charred orange, the morning heat already scorching. He high-steps back through the main passageway so that his toes don't burn, scurrying past the stormy cave entrance that huffs like a stoked blaze. He descends quickly into the lower chambers of the cave, the stinging light and driving wind to his back, and when he crawls into the shallow cave he discovers the fire has died completely.

Sky moves in a crouch to be near the cooler stone floor.

Teller? says Sky to the melted darkness, before he halts to listen, to adapt his eyes to the dim.

The sound of irregular breathing. It comes from deeper inside the cave, where the pot of wash water is resting. The heavy, bucket-sized pot contains the boiled ocean water they use for cleaning, the water sterile though too salty to drink, but Teller has dragged himself closer to it anyway. If he wants to drink that salty water, thinks Sky, then Teller's mind is no longer working.

The swinging handle of the pot has cooled enough to touch, so Sky waddles the large pot around the sound of Teller's increased panting, into the tunnel toward the others. The handle squeaks loudly enough that Mark calls out to him from the blackness.

Move slower, shouts Mark. You're going to break it.

Sky draws out his steps, gliding the pot gently.

Why did you bring the wash water? Mark asks when Sky finds a flat ledge to balance the pot.

Teller was—

Teller's hoarse breath, his dry tongue clicking against his teeth. Clenched and searching fists.

—Teller said Tie would need it, says Sky finally.

Tie, says Mark, we need to move you.

It'll start hurting again, Tie whispers.

It's going to get worse before it gets better.

Just a little longer, says Tie. Finish the story of three kings.

It's not important anymore, says Mark.

Important, thinks Sky. Vital is a container filled with withered bits of food and seven jars of water. But Important is Tie and Baby, Teller in the upper cave praying to Moth for water, and Green trying to take the Dark Sickness away.

Just remember me tomorrow.

Green would want the story, says Sky aloud, surprised at the strangeness of Green's name in his mouth, like a dot stamped on his tongue.

Tie inhales slow.

Green isn't here, says Mark flatly.

A dead silence expands, carrying responsibility and guilt and sorrow. Sky quickly speaks again.

Green said stories made living easier.

Tie slowly exhales.

One, she says suddenly.

One what? asks Mark.

It's my turn in the counting game, she says. If it's going to be my last story, I want to hear the end. I want to hear it even if it hurts—

Don't talk like that, says Mark.

You're the one who wanted to talk about Teller—

All right, all right, just—I'll tell it, says Mark in a rush. I guess I had seven fingers raised, and we were at the part where the first king died.

Then start outside the second city, says Tie impatiently.

Outside the second city, stammers Mark, outside the second city, the progeny brought the thirsty people water from the first city. So it was said they could create water from nothing.

Instead of raising a finger in darkness, Tie says Two.

Inside the second city, says Mark with a slower voice, the progeny opened the rich people's homes, allowing the starving people to enter. So it was said the progeny could cure all hunger.

Cure—a Green word. It pops the air, sticks in Sky's throat like a gasp of hope. A cure to make living easier, to return Teller's low and steady storytelling. Tie cured and running powerful down the bluffs. Green's bonfire lit again. Even as Sky wills the word to life, the waking truth, like an empty water drum, pries his heart wide.

Tie says Three quietly, as though speaking to herself.

And when the progeny reached the second king, says Mark, who was covered in the smell of the stolen perfume, they called out the name of the first man, waking first life.

Atom, said the progeny. Split.

And the perfume answered the call, says Mark. The perfume on the second king split his skin, ripping him apart.

The story staggers to a halt and then Mark says, I've got eight fingers raised now.

Tie nudges Sky with her ankle, motioning his turn in the counting game.

One, says Sky, lifting his pointer finger into the darkness before remembering no one can see it. Not Tie or Mark next to him, not Teller in the cave above—not Green. The hopelessness opens his heart wider, making him greedy for stories, for any cure at all.

Outside the third city, continues Mark, the people listened to the progeny until everyone spoke as one. So it was said the progeny was of the people.

Two, says Sky urgently.

Inside the third city, says Mark, the progeny were given the power of kings, and they spoke for so many years that their hair turned white. So it was said the progeny could not die.

Sky forces himself to say Three, and then feels his part in the counting game drift by. The story shoves coldly past him with its pretend, deathless progeny, reminding him only of what words can't cure.

And finally one day, says Mark, when messengers arrived with the gift of oil, the progeny, who had forgotten the Nations of the World, called out the name of the first man, waking first life.

Atom, said the progeny. Divide.

And the oil answered the call, says Mark. The oil began to glow and it grew so bright that all the people and the entire city disappeared, leaving nothing but red earth.

The hush afterwards lengthens, squeezing into the places Sky thought hope was supposed to live. When Mark speaks again, he is hurrying to a finish.

That makes nine fingers on my hands, he says. My last finger is for the gods, because then Moth flew into the sky.

Another quiet moment passes. Three breaths—four. Mark's voice sharpens.

I don't know what this has to do with the thing I found in the tide pools.

Tie speaks with a slow, hard voice.

Even if it's a gift from the gods, then we can't forget who we are and what we need to do. Gifts didn't help those people, and they won't help us. That's what the story means.

A low-hanging silence, then the sound of Mark's movements. A shuddering exhale from Tie.

Ready to move? asks Mark, and Sky stands to lift Tie's legs. One, two, three.

Although Tie cringes when Mark and Sky lift her, she does not cry out. Mark shuffles backwards toward the bottom of the narrow tunnel, Sky hobbling forward until he has to stoop low into the sleeping chamber. The air in the little cave is only slightly cooler than the air above, but when Sky settles Tie onto her side, so she can rest against the smooth and bowled stones of the floor, Sky feels the cool dampness of the ground like bone-deep relief. The chilled rocks feel the way Vital should, solid and lasting.

The moment Tie settles with a pained gasp, Mark's footsteps are back in the tunnel.

Get the wash water, he says to Sky, and he only just places the wash water safely in the sleeping chamber when he hears Mark's voice raised in the cave above.

Where's Teller? he shouts.

Guilt and dread—it returns to strangle Sky. Tie asks

him a question he does not hear. He is running up the tunnel and crouching among the shadowed corners of the cave with Mark, searching in the darkness for Teller.

Where did he go? asks Mark again, but a thought hits Sky in the stomach and he's scrambling into the main passageway, ducking his face away from the fiery breath of the cave entrance, the plastic cords on his feet sizzling against the cooked stones. Teller alone, empty and thirsty in the quiet loneliness—I left him alone with the Dark Sickness.

The tall tunnel to the storeroom smells differently than when Sky passed through it before. The first part of the tunnel is thick with the smell of burning hair, but near the end there is a distinct sweatiness, a dense wetness. When Sky steps into the storeroom and pauses to listen, he can hear it just faintly, No, quiet but fast, shallow but it is there—irregular breathing.

As Sky rushes to loosen the brick from the wall, he already fears the worst. Teller's naked skin scalded and bleeding where he dragged himself across the baked stones of the main passageway, his hair curled up and scorched against his skull. In Sky's mind, Teller's melted fists have slammed through the plastic lid of the container and all seven of the water jars are empty, all of the roots gone. Teller will croak his lies of determination and hope when the light falls on him, because the food has awakened his body, the water loosened his jaw, and he will look at Sky with wide, irresponsible eyes and be unable to speak for himself ever again.

But the light from outside winks red into the

storeroom, and for a long moment Sky cannot draw air into his lungs. His mind is slow to take in what is before him, the real merging with the untrue images in his mind. The inflamed burn wounds on Teller's sprawled body are seeping, yes, but he has also buried his seared toes and fingers into the liquid mud of the storeroom. The plastic container has not been disturbed, but lying next to Teller's twitching body is an entire water drum capsized, all of its contents being sucked quickly into the ground. Sky feels the softness underfoot, the muddy soil between his toes, and as Mark's quick footsteps in the tunnel beat closer, Sky shuts his eyes. He shuts out Teller and the empty drum and Mark is there, screaming Waste and Save it, the walls of Sky's mind swirling with shadow writing and the dead and the past and we are alone—the darkness cares nothing for us.

CHAPTER SIX

Under his vibrating shock, Sky knows he is helping Mark drag Teller's thrashing body through the main passageway. Teller's thighs and chest are rippled with blisters, white sores ringed purple and cracked in the centers. His grip on the leaking welts of Teller's knees must be painful, nerve wrenching, but Sky does not let go—cannot order his fingers to let go. His own feet must be scorched as well, though there is only a dull throb in his heels. The blazing sunlight steams through Mark's hair, the wet trails on Mark's cheeks flash, but Sky does not hear the words shouted from Mark's lips. As he carries Teller into the lower caves and drops the jerking pile into the shadows, Sky's mind is sunk to the mud between his toes and fingers, the lush sludge that has already dried on his skin and started to crack.

Mark is pointing furiously at the smoking cords on Sky's feet, so he unwraps the bands from his sore toes—disconnecting himself—and watches as Mark uses the cords to bind Teller's ankles and wrists into a gathered bunch. With his arms and legs fastened behind his back,

Teller can only rock his arched body into small leaps, tugging at the knots. His ribs pump air quickly and his throat is working below his clenched teeth, but Sky's mind still ranges nothing, everything around him a slow disquiet.

Then Mark is in the tunnel, hurrying toward Tie. Sky follows him into the darkness with motions stalled and shadow-trailed. The sensation reminds him of treading water in the ocean, filth and garbage floating all around him, and for a moment his ringing deafness feels like stillness. His mind detaches from his strange limbs, his white anxiety, like he has drifted into a different cave, like he is hearing a story. None of it is real, he remembers Mark saying, none of it is true.

But then Sky feels trembling against the hairs of his neck, the sensation of words being shouted into the darkness and bouncing back at him from the cave walls. This will be no talk to escape into, he knows. This will be no secret story written in clay.

The volume around Sky rises. Words register as pulsing gulps in his mind.

He's killed us, Mark shouts.

Be quiet, yells Tie. Be quiet.

Mark chokes a scream, or maybe a sob. He shouts louder. He's killed us all.

Stop, yells Tie, you're not helping. Just think, think—

Teller's not going to stop, hurries Mark. He's not thinking, he'll keep going to the storeroom—

—just need to think, what can we do—

We, what do you mean we? shrieks Mark. How would either of you know what to do? I've been doing everything all summer—

Stop, please, says Tie. This hurts, it hurts, be quiet—

You think this hurts? yells Mark. Think how much it's going to hurt when we're out of water, when the roots stop growing—

Mark gasps at heaped sobs. The throbbing in Sky's head tells him he's been holding his breath.

We're all going to die, says Mark.

Stop, says Tie like a moan. Just tell me how much water is left.

Not enough, snarls Mark, and the rain is too many days away.

Then, says Tie, you'll just have to set up the fog net sooner.

The storms will destroy it and then we'll have no fog net either, yells Mark, especially if you're not strong enough to help fix it.

The evaporation jars—

—barely enough for one person—

Then—then will there be enough water, says Tie, if Baby and I are gone?

What are you talking about? says Mark in a high voice.

Will there be enough?

There's enough for, I don't know, a few people, stutters Mark. We started with enough water for six. The last of it might get some of us past the storms—

Then just wait, says Tie in a flat voice. The problem will solve itself.

I told you, says Mark, his voice rising again, you're not going to die. It's Teller that's dying, he's been dying all summer, and now we can't trust him. He's going to keep trying for the water—

In the darkness, Mark's breath is coming fast.

There's no other way.

Sky's ears are completely open.

We need to help Teller die, says Mark.

Those aren't words, whispers Tie.

We have to—

Can't do that, says Tie louder.

He's dying, shouts Mark, and he's using our water to do it. He's killing us as he dies—

Teller's our friend, says Tie, her words rearing. He helped take care of you when you were a child, he tells us stories when we're scared—

Be quiet, says Mark.

—he used to give you his food when you missed Mother—

Shut your mouth, screams Mark between his pacing footsteps. He's going to die no matter what, we're going to miss him no matter what—

—he's not dead, Mark—

He's dying. He doesn't know who he is and he's suffering. We would be helping him and helping ourselves.

We can't do that to him, says Tie.

It will be the same as when Green put Little One out to sea.

No breath in the cave, only sharp, prickling memories.

That's not the same at all.

How, how is that not the same, Tie? says Mark and his pacing stops. Little One was born dying, she was dying with Song, and now Teller is suffering.

He's still alive, Mark. We can't just push Teller out to sea while he's still alive.

The ocean's already killed him, hurries Mark. He was dead the moment he cut his foot, he's been a waste of water and food ever since—

No, says Tie.

Listen to me, says Mark. We have no choice—

No, says Tie louder.

Green would do it, pushes Mark. He'd do it because he'd have no choice.

Tie sobs.

We don't have a choice either, says Mark quieter.

The darkness inhales.

Sky, says Tie, what do you think?

Sky's stomach twists into his throat. The word Teller is slippery and sick in his mouth.

Sky, if you're going to help carry Teller to the beach, you need to agree to this. This has to be your choice, too.

His mind screams silently at the blackness, at the Vital mud in the storeroom, between his toes, Responsibility and Shouldn't, shouldn't have let the ocean climb—

This is important, says Tie louder. Sky, you aren't a baby anymore. You need to say something.

This is stupid, says Mark. He doesn't know what we need.

Sky, yells Tie, her pained gasps quickening. You won't get another chance. You need to speak now.

His tongue burns with stomach acid. Eyes flared to the underground darkness.

Sky, shouts Tie.

Useless, snarls Mark as he moves around the cave. I'll do it myself.

What are you going to do? says Tie at once.

I'm going to finish Teller quickly, shouts Mark.

The pounding of a fist on a bare chest.

I'm going to kill Teller right now.

Teller, weeps Tie.

There's nothing left to discuss, shouts Mark. This has to happen. We have to do this.

Tie sobs.

I know, she says.

Footsteps in the tunnel.

Sky's chest thumps, his legs moving quicker than his thoughts, seeking out noises in the tunnel above—the float of Mark's voice in the upper cave. Sky's feet are numb underneath his body, working on their own to search out the words he cannot speak.

And slowly, like a rising hum, Mark's stammering breaks through to Sky's mind.

Teller, I have to, have to—

Mark's words are fast, desperate, a shouted whisper pressed into a long whine.

Has to happen, do you understand? Like Green did for Song and Little One, I have to, don't want to but have to, we love you, I love you—

Shadows blink about the cave—Mark darting in and out of the red morning light drifting down from the main passageway. Sky's toes creep him into view of Teller's lurching knees and Mark's muddy fingers gripping the heaviest object within reach—the strange, wooden globe from the tide pools. Standing over Teller, Mark's eyes and mouth are full moons, Responsibility fixed below the globe raised high over his head. Mark inhales a gasp that rips the air from Sky's chest, and with his entire lunging weight, Mark drives the globe downward.

Bone cracks under split flesh. A sucking sound as Mark lifts the globe from Teller's snorting face. The chopping repeats—a clap, clap, crunch that flattens Teller's nose, crushes his liquid mouth, broken groans wrenching open Sky's plugged ears, his flared eyes that must Look—can't look, can't, my Friend, my whole life shrieking Please, should not have, should not have to Kill him, please—Kill him quicker.

The striking ends suddenly with a pop—the globe cracks in two against Teller's face. Pebbles inside the globe spill across the stone floor with the sound of rain, sticking against the red of Teller's cracked cheeks and caved teeth. The gurgling in Teller's throat—it slowly drowns as silent, unsuccessful coughs, his lungs attempting to clear their fluids behind a collapsed jaw. His body tries for five more soundless breaths, five more agonies to save itself, and the sixth breath pulls in nothing but shivering, a trembling that increases, quakes and jolts, before it slackens.

The halves of the globe clink and roll to the floor below Mark's weaving knees. His thick arms are limp, his feet turned inward. This child, Sky's mind whispers, this stranger. When Mark slumps to the ground and curls up on his side, Sky does not immediately understand the rattling noise from Mark's mouth, his chest inhaling, reeling up for a cry, and when the sobs do come, they shriek and shudder throughout the caves.

Have to do everything, cries Mark. Don't want to, don't want, should not have, not have—

The repeating words—they are Sky's, his unspoken answers for Tie. From Mark's wet and twisted mouth, the begging is just as useless—too late to change anything, the words Forever as weak as damp clay. Teller's crumpled mouth empties itself drip by drip, becoming a hollow Mark's noise cannot fill, and as the heaviness of the mistake fills the shadows, Sky loses his chance to speak, to Confess, his words for Teller always and from now on missing.

CHAPTER SEVEN

Don't want to, don't do it—

Mark's body tightens around Teller's crushed head, his clouded pupils begged open and staring at split flesh. The heat of the late morning presses into Sky's lungs, his burnt feet feel coated with stinging rubber, but he does not rise from the ground. He continues to shiver and listen to Mark moaning.

—don't do it, can't do it—

Sky does not know how long he stares at Teller's still, dirty feet, or what finally drifts his fingers to Teller's toes, then to Mark's shaking shoulders. Perhaps if he turns Mark's face away from the red sight, Mark will stop trembling. The thought inspires no weight in Sky's mind. Maybe then, thinks Sky, Mark will stop whispering quickly to himself, pleading, but Sky has never known how to do such a thing—to move Mark from his grief. Instead, he begins to untie the cords from Teller's wrists and ankles with clumsy twitches as his mouth works up to a whisper.

Mark? Sky asks carefully.

Mark sobs so loudly that surprise lurches from Sky's

throat. At the sound of Sky's voice, Mark weeps wide and without restraint, his ribs pressing out cries that eject Sky from the chamber, sending him fleeing into the tunnels. It is only after he drops lower into the caves that Sky realizes Tie is calling out to him.

Is that you? her voice echoes.

He rushes down into the sleeping chamber. In the wrung darkness, Tie's quickened breaths feel uncomfortably near, a tightened core of inhales rolling deeper and more unstable than before.

Tell me, says Tie between gasps. Is Teller—

To talk to her, to lift up the words, would be to lift boulders, so Sky only drops near Tie, kneeling so close he can feel which muscles in her crooked legs and hips are gripped in pain and which have given up. She is not weeping, though. She is not lost like Mark. She is not still and empty like Teller.

Teller, Sky finally whispers. Poor Teller.

Sky escapes next to Tie's hard stomach, curling up small.

But her sweaty hands find his arms. Sharp fingers cut into his wrists. Sky yelps.

Tell me, Tie bursts. Is Teller dead?

Sky nods in the darkness, trying to jerk his wrists away. Yes is the word he finally stutters.

Her fingernails dig deeper.

We had to do it, says Tie in rush. There was no other way. If you knew another way, you should have said something.

A strange, juddering sob pops from Sky's mouth as she shakes him.

Why didn't you say something? You're not a child—there's no one to take care of you, do you hear me? Green's dead, Teller's dead—everything's dead.

Mark, says Sky remembering suddenly. Mark's crying.

A flash of pain across Sky's face—Tie's unseen hand slapping him. Mark has struck him many times, in the darkness and in the light, in front of the others, but he has never been hit by Tie.

Do you hear me? she shouts with flecks of spit. There's no one to help you.

Tie's voice cracks into a groan. Her fingers loosen.

Leave, go away, she cries in pain. Leave me alone.

His terrified body combs through the tunnels, back into the heat.

In the dim cave above, Mark's crumpled form still has not moved and his cries have not quieted. Teller's crushed skull has grown a dark pool, his body making room for poison. Sky's terror grows flush with the cave walls, the Dark Sickness thirsty and panting and close despite a droning responsibility telling him Teller's body needs to be moved or it will poison them, Mark needs to help Tie or her body will kill her, they need food and water or they will die, food and water, food and water—

The white cold of fear—Sky wants to burn it away but he can't, can't get warm, even as he turns into the burning daylight. In the main passageway, with the heat reaching up through his blistered feet, he scrambles on all fours over the tunnel's coarse stones, toward the glowing storeroom—the brick was not replaced in the wall and dust swirls through the open rectangle. Crouched low, Sky gropes the surface of the floor, its muddy surface already hardening in the dry air, parts of the ground molded into the shapes of Teller's limbs. The depressions show the outline of a body, Teller's life summed up by a gathering of forms trapped in the dirt. Elbow and toe gouges—these leavings no more alive than dust, no louder than writing in clay. Even as the marks ask to be read, the lines of Teller's dragged fingertips crumble when Sky touches them, the sand collapsing into the round pits made by Teller's shoulders, shoulders Sky used to ride to the beach. The earth oozes a hungry smell as Sky fails to keep Teller alive this way, to remember his remains by touch—even this Sky manages to ruin. Near the impression that must be Teller's head there is the faintest indent of a mouth, barely open, Teller's words made as filthy and silent as dirt, a hollow ready to let the poison in.

Handfuls of mud—Sky smears them up and down his shaking legs that aren't strong enough to stop anything, across his needy stomach and throat, and covers his face with sludge, jagged bits of rock and grit scouring his mouth that causes death by saying nothing, a voice that killed to be born but might as well be dead for all its quiet. Sky rolls in the mud of the storeroom where Teller's body used to be, in the warm dampness that feels only half-alive. The dust thickens until it breaks Sky's chest with coughing, finally laying his convulsing body flat, but the marks on the floor are already ruined, only vaguely human, unrecognizable bodies, many bodies, all lost and swallowed by the past.

Hollows, Sky sobs. Their caved bodies, their mouths, the writing—hollows within hollows. Teller's mouth—it might be Sky's mouth, and the caked mud on Sky's face cracks open, to imitate the hollow of Teller's mouth. Around Sky, written in the oldest clay of the walls, are also round shapes, scratches like circles, orbs. Like eyes, or like open mouths. Sky forms his lips into their dead shape and makes a sound.

Oh is the sound from Sky's tongue, his lips shaped like the circles on the walls.

Curiosity, like a small, blue light, gently cools his mind.

Oh, Sky decides, the circular symbol on the wall is an Oh. It makes an Oh sound, its meaning and shape one and the same.

And realization—it makes every scratch on the wall capable of sound, every written word ripe with voice. The voice is still muddled and low like his own, but the writing on the walls, all of it stands up, ready to speak, like it has been waiting all this time, all these years. The words become hollows that carry voices, like bowls hold water, like bodies hold stories and memories and families—is this the way I'm supposed to keep you? thinks Sky through smiling tears. Can I hope to keep them now?

Hope, says Sky aloud, a word with Oh in it. At least one hollow filled with voice, filled with something besides poison, taking away the Nothingness. There are no cures now for Teller's prayers and Green's storeroom sobbing, but determination and hope, relief from the Dark Sickness, stories to push the poison out—this is what Teller meant by Vital—I can keep them forever this way.

Sky quickly closes off the storeroom with the brick and rushes back through the blaze of the main passageway, his arms flattening his steaming hair, protecting his lowered face, and for the first time that day he truly considers the cooked state of his feet. Any more running today, Sky knows, will rupture the blisters and sickness can climb up my legs like it climbed into Teller—I need Mark's legs to help me.

But when he reaches Mark knotted tightly near Teller's body, his strong limbs coiled up so small with a weakness so much like his own, the word Oh becomes a support beam, a doorway, an Opening. Mark so helpless, useless—is this how Mark has always seen me?

Mark, begs Sky. Please get up.

Mark's puffy eyes are squeezed shut, his head shaking back and forth.

Can't, cries Mark. Can't kill Teller, can't do it alone—

Sky stirs his voice again, awakening it.

Teller's dead, says Sky firmly.

Mark weeps and rocks his body.

Can't take care of Teller, sobs Mark. Can't take care of Mother or Green or Song—

He's circling, thinks Sky with Oh still in mind. A spiraling death guilt, the same Sky feels for Mother—this he now shares with Mark. If Sky wanted to hurt his brother, to split his grief wide, then Sky would tell Mark the pain is never hollow. Shove work into the emptiness made by the missing pieces, try to replace mothers with brothers, but the Forever writing does not fade and the questions do not stop itching. Above all, the Dark Sickness does not disappear, death does not stop coming, not for Teller, not for Green or Mother.

Not for Tie.

Sky's heart trips. There will be more death soon if I don't remember Teller's words. Get Mark working, think of Teller's body and the water supply later—right now, I have to take care of Tie.

Mark, says Sky suddenly, I'm going to help Tie and you have to help me.

No, whines Mark, but the new hardness of Sky's voice forces Mark's eyes open. A bloodshot red surrounds the fogged Ohs of Mark's eyes, both pupils revolving upward and finally fixing on Sky.

Mark jumps into a sitting position.

What? gasps Mark, and Sky touches the caked earth on his face. Looking down, he sees the rest of his body discolored with hardened mud, so Sky begins knocking the crusted dirt off his limbs in chunks and clouds. Under the shell, his skin feels powdery and smooth. His chest expands wide. His muscles round as dust coats the wet of Teller's face—a gentle burial. Mark watches Sky like a plant growing quickly out of the ground, delivering itself from the earth, and with Mark's full attention, Sky's limbs feel able, his back tall and strong.

Don't worry about the storeroom right now, says Sky slapping his hands clean. Can you take Teller outside?

Outside, repeats Mark.

Yes, and make a fire—we're going to need light to help Tie. Can you do that?

Mark sits up and nods quickly with an enthusiasm Sky recognizes—his own childish actions reflected back at him. Mark begins gently arranging Teller's body, head ducked and actions so cautious that Sky sees the way he has always obeyed Mark's orders—so eager to do right, so eager to erase wrongs. And Sky knows Tie was correct, that Mark can't take care of anyone anymore. He has no determination or hope left—it's my turn now to help everyone.

So sorry, Mark whispers softly in no direction, in every direction. With careful, limping steps, Sky descends into the lower caves, into the thick and inky blackness that presses against his eyes, his ears searching and stretching for Tie. Soon he can make out her breathing low in the sleeping chamber, her groans of pain straining against the stones. When he enters the cave, he stops cold.

Oh, she cries.

His word, his hope—it is alive and hurting Tie. A circular figure that Sky filled with voice, like Tie's round body filled with Baby. Writing dies if no one remembers its voice and Teller said Baby has to make sound—Baby has to cry right after.

Tie, says Sky sitting near her raised and parted knees.

I'm going to die, says Tie gasping through gritted teeth. It hurts all the time now.

I've got the wash water ready, says Sky, and Mark is bringing light—

Going to die, repeats Tie. Oh—going to die—

Sky reaches out to Tie's flexed and sticky arms, to her fists gripped near her hips. The bowled stones under her back are slick with her sweat, and when he retrieves a boiled strip of tarp from the wash bucket to mop her face, she pulls it into her clawing fingers. A ripping sound.

Dying—no water—

Tie, listen to me, says Sky. You won't die because, because—

—Green—going to die—

What would Teller say? thinks Sky. What would Green say?

—because you're special, says Sky. Remember the mother story? Only mothers bring us out of the cave.

Tie continues breathing quickly, but her words stop and Sky can feel her listening.

Yes, says Sky quickly, that's what Green used to say—

Oh, says Tie with more pain than realization, but Sky hears the word Oh doubling itself between his mouth and her belly, spinning his thoughts faster.

The Twin Goddesses, says Sky. Remember?

I don't care, Tie weeps. I want Green. I want to die like Green.

No—

What if, sobs Tie, what if Green didn't fall?

Tie, Green's gone—

What if he jumped?

Green's body dropping across the cliff face—Sky sees it all again, scorched into the back of his mind, repeating—Green, his legs, Green falling, the tide pools. Green's eyes closed when telling Song's stories, his hands releasing Little One into the sea and his weeping in the storeroom afterwards, fingertips tracing silent words in clay, No swimming away from here—

Fear jaws the inside of Sky's chest as Oh flickers in his heart, hope falling away with Green, dragging the stories, the voices and names, into darkness. Cold and distant, as Mark described Green long ago at the bonfire, when Tie demanded the truth, the memory of Green's arms floating away from Sky's swimming body—

And all the while, Teller insisting on vital memories, on determination and hope.

Sky raises his voice into a shout.

Tie, listen to me. Green's dead—we're all dead, really dead—if there's no one left to remember us. If you want Green, then you have to stay alive and remember him tomorrow.

Just remember me tomorrow, whispers Tie, drenching Sky with a glowing sadness, Green momentarily sprung to life through her voice. Tie inhales in one long pull, and exhales a deep, moaning sob, her mourning filling up her whole shuddering body. Sky understands her only in half-words, but pieced together, he hears Hurts and Dying and Miss him so much.

So sorry, says Sky reaching out to the shredded rag in her hands. Tie, I know you're strong enough. That's how the Twin Goddesses made mothers. You're strong enough to bear it.

Tie takes a lasting inhale and a shaking exhale.

—listening, she says at last.

Sky exhales a deep, quaking breath. So many new words ejected from his trapped up tongue, but when he speaks again, Tie's fingers fasten around his, driving his voice forward.

You only have to remember, says Sky. Remember what Green said, how the Twin Goddesses made the first people? They made people like them.

Two heads, says Tie between inhales. Four arms, four legs—

And everyone rolled around the world like wheels, says Sky. They made canyons and mountains to catch rain. Trees sprung from their tears. They made the world grow.

Tie spurts a cold laugh. Spit mists the air.

You believe that? sneers Tie, and Sky pauses to think, about Teller who prayed to Moth, and about Mark who says it's all lies. Untrue things happen in stories, Sky knows, but that doesn't mean they aren't memories.

I believe, answers Sky, that Green told the story this way.

Another trembling moment, and Tie nudges Sky to continue.

The world grew green, says Sky, but the Twin Goddesses grew afraid. There were too many people, so the Twin Goddesses split everyone in half to slow them down. That's why the progeny have two legs, two arms, and one head, and only mothers are like the Twin Goddesses when it's time for babies to be born, becoming two heads, four arms, and four legs once again.

Just as Sky's skin ripples, thrilled to air so many words at once, Tie groans. Her body clenches abruptly, as though to lift some unseen object. Her knees jab Sky as they part wider, and still clawing his fingers, her hands drag to her stomach, to her hips, and Sky can feel her muscles twisting. The stench of human waste fills the cave.

Mark, we need light, Sky shouts up the tunnel before turning back to Tie.

Tie, I'll clean you. Teller said everything needs to be clean—what can I do?

Her red grip nearly crushes Sky's knuckles.

Keep, stutters Tie. Something—

Keep talking? tries Sky while yanking his fingers from her clutch. After retrieving another shredded piece of tarp from the pot of wash water, Sky begins wiping her sweltered face in nervous jerks, pushing her damp hair out of her eyes, and he starts bathing her from her face downward.

It was not long, says Sky with a shaking voice, before the progeny were jealous of mothers.

Jealous, says Tie bitterly, the word spit from her lips as Sky sponges her slack arms to her gritty palms, washes away the thick smell of her underarms, hesitant to move the cloth to her chest grown bulged and tense.

Green said they were jealous, says Sky as he works. It's why people started controlling mothers. The world was filling with so many jealous people that the Twin Goddesses had to split everyone in half again.

Sky pauses, stops washing the sandy creases at Tie's hips and listens. In the blackness of the tunnel are other breaths—a faint smoky smell.

Mark? says Sky, his frustration climbing. Where's the light?

Don't want to control mothers, whines Mark from the darkness. Didn't want to control life and death, should not have—

Please, shouts Sky in a high-cracked voice. Just bring some light.

Footsteps scurrying up the tunnel. Waste, thinks Sky, a waste of energy. Have I been this same burden on the others?

Tie's breath—it piles into shallow gasps.

Mothers, says Tie. Moth—

Moth? asks Sky and realizes what she's saying.

Moth, right, yes, says Sky as he washes around Tie's thighs and knees. Mothers were—were split in half again, and one half was Moth. Moth flew into the sky, taking her children with her. The other half was Bear who slept in a cave. Her children slept in caves too, in the cave of her stomach. Now mothers fill the world by hollowing themselves—only mothers can bear people out of the cave.

Green, cries Tie mournfully, her muscles slack. So hollow and unhappy—

No, not hollow, pleads Sky, the washrag dropping from his hands as he gestures frantically. Not hollow, not to me. Green was—he's like our words, he's alive this way, and you're like Bear—we're in this cave—

Cave—out—

You have to bear it, begs Sky, to bring you and Baby out of it.

Out of the cave, says Tie. Oh.

Mark, Sky yells. Get here now.

And glancing over his shoulder, Sky sees yellow firelight glowing high in the tunnel.

CHAPTER EIGHT

Light bobs into the sleeping chamber so burning Sky blinks rapidly to protect his eyes, everything underground diminished to a flickering pain. At first, Mark is only bodiless legs below intense brightness, but gradually Sky can see the dusty drips trailing his own arms, the mud still caked in the folds of his elbows. Even more slowly, Sky understands Tie as slashes of browns—the shining brown of her washed stomach heaving and rising, her flushed and staring face leaned back against the bowled stones of the cave, and the dark, wet brown on the ground beneath her, dripped sweat turning to mud.

And when Mark crouches near, his lit torch lowers to the ground, and the space between Tie's legs brightens.

Panic crashes open Sky's mind.

Can't, whispers Mark. The word hangs vaguely in the air, hovering Tie.

With a wrenching effort, Sky tears his attention from the bulging pressure between Tie's legs and looks back at Mark, his stunned face shaking back and forth, his clouded eyes flared wide to the Dark Sickness.

Can't do it, says Mark, repeating. Can't take care of Tie or Teller—

Teller, whispers Tie to no one, to the Dark Sickness pressing down.

Hold the light here, Sky finally orders Mark, but what he thinks is Waste while wiping the soiled ground underneath Tie with the rag. Careful to keep his hands clean, he pitches the wad toward the far corner of the cave and retrieves a fresh strip of tarp. This isn't all bodies give us, Sky repeats to himself, not only waste and sickness and pain, but also memories and stories and Tie's body is holding Baby.

If we get through this, says Sky quickly, I promise we'll remember Teller. I promise you his stories, I promise—

Sky continues pitching words into the black void of the cave as he fetches a new rag to clean Tie's upper thighs, hesitantly moving closer to her groin. His shadow trips so often into the torchlight the most he knows is how swollen and stretched Tie's become, radiating a heat that frightens him—is this bad, is this fever? There's liquid, slippery, something dangerous—is this poison? But Teller said—

And then darkness. A choking sob.

Mark, hold the light still, demands Sky.

A cry from Tie grates open, her body clenches, and at the same time the roundness between her legs grows, pushing back against the rag in Sky's hand.

His hand snaps back like he's been burned.

Oh—out, says Tie through clenched teeth. Out—

You want us out? asks Sky, but Tie only hisses angrily,
her breath sucked in quickly. The firelight wobbles closer.
Blood mists out of her skin where it stretches thin.

Darkness.

Mark, I told you, hold the light—

The torch jumps high again. A bulb pushes from Tie—
hairs between hairs. A forehead.

The light dips.

Mark, Sky screams.

Tie screams at her stomach.

The light jerks high again, and there are small shoulders kinked between Tie's legs—Tie gasps another
shriek—a bundle of tight limbs drop wet and warm into
Sky's shaking hands. For an instant Sky's amazement at
the strange weight of the baby, the lightness of head and
torso, numbs him to the fact that the limbs aren't moving.
There's no movement, no sound—Teller said Baby has to
cry right after—

But as Sky turns the crooked figure in his hands, firelight passes over the new face, and two clear eyes slice open
beneath tight eyelids. A small cough. Narrow hips the
width of a fist, flinching legs, waking fingers—they clench
and sprout a high-pitched whine. Wet and shivering fists,
a dark circle in the center of a wrinkled face—Oh, it cries,
creaking and rough, Oh, Sky repeats back to it, smiling,
relief like cool water, all around him, swimming in the
ocean with Green, his arms lifting and supporting Baby,
alive and crying—

—crying for something, louder, needs something, What do I do? Little legs tangled in a wet rope, it's attached to the stomach, attached to Tie—

Tie. Her breath rolls deeper now, face pointing at the cave ceiling, twisted for a final groan. Pink sweat drips into the bowled stones of the floor, and then a knot of cords follows out of her.

Blood, gasps Mark, his knuckles clapped to his bared teeth. Poison.

I don't know—I don't think so, says Sky quietly, his eyes tracing back to Baby's slight stomach. Teller said not all blood is poison.

Mark's face pales, looks away, and Sky carries Baby and the corded sack to the bucket of wash water, moves a new wash rag gently over Baby's scrunched face, between the slight, folded limbs. As he washes the strange bundle, he is reminded of the inside of his cheeks and the underside of his tongue, but Baby's small palms are more familiar, fingers pulled into weak fists that tremble open as she bawls, shaking—she is a She.

When Sky carries Baby to Tie, the lit torch has tipped low and Mark is gently petting Tie's hair.

Please don't die, whispers Mark.

Dead? asks Tie, with confused tears leaking into her hair. Green, I'm so sorry, she pleads. I don't want to die.

She is still whispering when she rounds her arm, as Sky brings Baby close, wails still ejecting from the small ribs. Propped in the crook of Tie's elbow, Baby's eyes slowly peer open, the thin cries finally curling into surprise at Tie's touch, her fingertips gently exploring feet never dirtied, knees never scraped, the fine, lopsided eyebrows unfurrowing. Slowly, Tie quiets Baby against her heart, and in their exhausted silence and the flickering dim, Sky's hands are empty again.

Sky asks, what should I do about—

But words fail to describe the rope still strung to Baby's stomach, the raw bundle now resting dark and wet at Tie's side.

Leave it, says Tie with eyes staring beyond the cave. Yours fell off later.

Sky's gaze traces the cord attached to the middle of Baby's stomach, then touches his navel, the protruding knot in the center of his own belly, an Oh mark in his skin, an Oh realized again in his mouth—we were all tied to the cave once.

The burning torch, now no more than a smoking plug in Mark's hand, dips, and this time Sky lets it, laying himself flat against the ground. The stones feel damp and cool, a smooth hollow accepts his body, a roundness—the round object Mark found in the tide pools. Instead of crushing Teller's skull, Tie is pulling the globe in half with her parting knees. Instead of spreading pebbles across a stone floor, seeds fall across Teller's muddy body, plants rising out of the wet so green, for Green, the life stings Sky's eyes and dries his mouth. Teller and Green and Mother—a buried memory of a mother's voice—remember me tomorrow.

Sky wakes from the dream with a dry throat and Baby's keening loud again, worry vibrating though his body only half-crawled from sleep. Edging through the blackness of the cave to Tie, feeling her ribs rise and fall, he lifts Baby from Tie's arms, disturbing a rich human smell. Sky grabs the last rag from the wash water to clean the waste between Baby's legs and from Tie's lap before replacing her tutting back in the bend of Tie's arm.

By that time, Sky's mouth and eyes are parched to sand. Even some of the blisters on his feet have wrinkled thin. Since Mark is still asleep and Baby has quieted, Sky elects himself to the storeroom, for water and for time to himself. Time to think, Green used to call it. The main passageway is black—it is long past sundown—and the summer storms have gasped themselves into a rare quiet, allowing a faint moonlight and a ground safe to walk. In the storeroom, Sky's fingers swap the loose brick for the glass shard, the dim light revealing once again the tipped-over water drum and the disturbed floor of dried mud. It makes the remaining water drum, the white hairs of the summer roots, and the closed container draped with tarps glow with the word Vital.

And the word Rich, thinks Sky, grateful for their remaining supplies. Carefully, Sky retrieves three roots from the buried container and a jar of drinking water, daily provisions, and before returning the brick to the wall, he finds himself staring once again at the old writing lit barely by the trickled starlight. He also examines Mark's counting symbols, eyeing the water left in the single drum. Counting back on his fingers, Three, Two, One—if one jar holds water for one day, can we survive the summer? Enough for twenty dormant days, maybe. Enough for Tie to get strong again, for them to try the fog net and the last of Green's evaporation jars. Mark knows the counting symbols best, but Sky sees fullness instead of emptiness, the voices of the past alive in clay, stored memories to drive them forward.

To the side of the water drum is a sharp piece of tin, the tool Mark uses for counting and tracking. The grip of Mark's counting tool narrows to a square point, for punching marks in the wall, so at the far end of the cave, where the simplest writing is stamped in clay, Sky makes an indent below Tie's name for Baby. With his littlest finger, he rounds the square impression into a circle, into an Oh. It makes Baby's name stands out from the rest. Special, thinks Sky, remembering Teller. Like mothers.

After closing off the storeroom from the outside, Sky finds his bright happiness too quickly at the pale entrance of the cave, listening to the distant shush of ocean waves, a fingernail of golden moon peeking from the south. Mark did as he was told—Teller's body is heaped just beyond the cave's mouth. In the night shadows, Teller's broken nose and sideways jaw appear coated with black, the long burn wounds up his stomach and thighs a splotched gray. His hardened muscles have latched his limbs at odd angles, upsetting Sky's memory of hands that used to reassure him and shoulders that used to support him, Teller's body reduced to a tangle of elbows and knees lit dimly by the stars.

And with the food and water held in his arms, his heart just moments ago filled with joy and hope, Sky is ashamed. His voice can still speak for itself, and it fills only with the words Teller gave him, who was given voice by Green before him and Song before him, Mother before her, and all the others who ever left their mark in the storeroom.

Determination and hope, says Sky, gripping the food and water and also the memories, grasping at the future that was given to him.

From the main passageway, leaving the warm nighttime air, Sky carries the roots and water jar low into the ground, into the tight sleeping chambers where Tie and Mark have awoken and are whispering quietly to each other.

So glad you're alive, says Mark to Tie.

His words—they turn without sourness, without wanting. They sound like Please. They feel like Peace.

Silently, Sky pushes the roots into Mark's hands that are still shaking, and Sky helps Tie recline so she can drink and eat with Baby asleep in her lap.

Thank you, Tie says afterwards, and it is her own voice speaking again.

After a number of silent sips, Sky breaks the quiet with a whisper.

We need to take Teller to the ocean, says Sky gently.

More slow breaths.

I want to be there, says Tie.

Not safe to move you, says Mark.

I have to know, says Tie.

To remember, thinks Sky, nodding in the darkness.

When at last he moves to take Baby and help Tie to her knees, Mark stands to lift her to her feet. With Tie's arm around Mark's neck, they all move so slowly toward the upper caves and rest so often that Baby only stirs once they reach the heat of the main passageway. By then, Tie's breath sharpens with every step, and settled against the wall of the cave entrance, the moonlight shows her face creased tight with pain.

Tie doesn't move, though it is a long time before Baby's anger from being awoken silences in Sky's arms, longer for Tie's pursed eyes to reopen, and even longer for them all to pull their stares from Teller's body knotted against the rocks.

So sorry, says Mark with a coiled whine, kneeling near Teller's feet. He repeats the words to Tie, to Teller, to the hot, cracked ground.

Sorry, thinks Sky. The word is the tiniest drop of water blinked into the sea, a gift to an Enemy Ocean never satisfied, always hungry.

Sky glances from Teller's body to the distant beach, measuring the ocean's wave up the sand. He guesses the moment when high tide's retreat will allow them to push Teller's body, like driftwood, out to sea, and Sky even opens his mouth to ask Mark about the tide, impulsively seeking Mark's orders.

But with Mark's face and eyes bent low to Teller, Sky notices how clouded Mark's eyes have become, from all the daytime work he's risked, alone while everyone else remained asleep underground. I don't want to do the work alone, Mark once said, but that's exactly what Sky and the others asked of him.

It's almost time, says Sky aloud, but wonders how much time is left until Mark is completely blind. It is past time, he knows, when Mark can take care of the work on his own. We will unravel the fog net tomorrow, knows Sky. We will haul the fabric out of the cave and I will repair the fog net while Mark takes care of Tie and Baby.

Tie finally speaks, reaching for Baby.

More than anyone else, she says, Teller would have wanted a eulogy.

When Sky returns his stare from the beach, both Mark and Tie are watching him. Baby's mouth is quiet against Tie's breast, but Tie and Mark are asking Sky something, begging him with their eyes.

Teller's favorite was the story of Moon and Bear, says Tie. He liked how the progeny spoke like us.

Tie stares out to sea then and Mark bows his face, unable to look at Teller without crying. With hesitant steps, Sky moves into the night, his fingers outstretched over Teller's body in the traditional way.

CHAPTER NINE

The story of Moon and Bear, says Sky, starts when the
Great Fires began—

His breath skips, the weight of the others' gazes crowding the air in his mouth. It was a promise he made low in
the caves, though, a promise spoken to everyone and to
himself, so Sky pushes his breath forward, finds it growing strong and steady as the words come—downhill stones
gathering speed. From Sky's own tongue, even as his child's
voice cracks high and low, Green's descriptions carry a sadness that shines and fills. For a floating moment, Teller's
rhythms and repetitions in his own mouth take Sky from
his thirsty grief, from the staggering age of the world and
its dangerous hunger.

When the Great Fires began and Moth flew into the
sky, continues Sky, the Enemy Ocean crawled over all the
cities and daylight died in smoke. Then the lights in Old
City went out and the Walking Stars stretched out of reach
and everything was very dark. But above the smoke, the
progeny circled the world on the back of Moth, and they
talked of a time when the world was young. The progeny

could live for a hundred years, so old their hair turned white, and since they had a lot of food and water and cures, they had the time to talk. They would wash themselves with drinking water, they would tell old stories, and they would remember the past.

There was Venus, says Sky, the name like a burning spark in his mind. Venus liked to talk about people caring for each other.

Do you know what love is? says Tie, murmuring the clever voice of Venus out of habit.

A beautiful thing? asks Mark, half-heartedly giving the response of the progeny, his words slightly high-pitched, the way Teller gave voice to the progeny to make everyone laugh. Mark sniffs his wet nose.

No, says Tie, giving Venus's answer. Love is the child of plenty and hunger, always learning and always wanting.

There was also Mars, says Sky, continuing the story. Mars liked to talk about people fighting—

—and about war, adds Sky, remembering Teller's word.

Do you know what a mushroom does? says Mark, his back straightening to give Mars a gruff voice.

A cloud weapon, thinks Sky, or at least that's what Green once told him. A plant from the Garden of the Gods, Song said years ago. Sky presses both memories together, but Mush Room still doesn't sound like a weapon or food to him.

Tie hitches her voice even higher than Mark's, playing the voices of the progeny.

It stops problems? squeaks Tie, and Mark bows a small smile.

No, says Mark, giving the answer of Mars. Mushrooms stop everything, good and bad.

But Moon, says Sky encouraged by the others, was the only one who spoke of Bear, about how the world below was dark and old and dying, how Bear was living in a cave while the progeny were safe with Moth, doing nothing to help.

So Moon grew lonely for Bear, says Sky. Moon told stories of Bear and deep down in her cave, under the faraway stars, Bear told stories about Moon to her children, when smoke hid them in darkness, when the cave was most lonely.

Lonely, remembers Sky, the word swirling the missing parts of the story, the hollows Teller would have filled with his low and powerful voice. Teller starting stories with his face raised to the ceiling of rock, ending with his head bowed—if Teller's mouth could speak, words would be vibrating against stone walls, ringing throughout the tunnels. If Teller was alive, he would still be praying, hoping for the progeny, for Moth to save them from a world dead everywhere but in his mind.

Poor Teller, thinks Sky. No caring Moon to remember him, the Dark Sickness turning his stories to responsibilities and whispers before begging hands and eyes, all of it demanding, every moment, his determination and hope.

Fists clenched, with Teller's body at his feet, Sky points his voice up into the nighttime, sending his words south, beyond the pale beach, the black mountain ridges, toward the bright haze surrounding a weak sliver of moon.

Finally Moon spoke, insists Sky, because in the beginning were words, creating something from nothing.

How do worlds begin? Sky asks, making Moon's question to the progeny low and serious.

Tie and Mark speak at the same time, sprouting a quiet happiness in Sky's chest.

With blood, says Mark, giving Mars's answer.

With love, says Tie, giving Venus's answer.

When Sky gives Moon's answer, he opens his dirty palms, the same way Teller used to open his hands whenever he told the story. Instead of raising them into the air, though, Sky places his palms on Teller's sticky chest and forehead. In this way, I will remember you, promises Sky. Words for you—not for Moon, not for Moth.

With light, says Sky, and the progeny watched as Moon jumped to the earth, determined to help Bear and let there be light.

Bear felt the world quake when Moon met the earth, says Sky as he stands. Bear rushed outside her cave and the first thing she saw, glowing in the darkness, was the round and shiny shape of Moon. At Moon's feet, a strange plant sprung up from the ground—

Baby coughs open a thin wail so suddenly Sky kneels near Tie while Mark hovers, eyebrows raised. Tie quickly readjusts Baby against her breast, her eyes darting and searching when Baby rejects her once, twice. The motion of Tie's arms turns to swaying then, slowly changing Baby's outrage into loud interest.

A flower, whispers Tie, correcting Sky as Baby's irritation trips into curiosity.

The plant was a flower, says Sky, pulling the story back to Teller. The flower was streaked with red when the full Moon gave it to Bear. When Bear took the flower, her stomach grew round and large, and it grew so large so quickly that Egg dropped from her body a moment later. When Egg hit the ground it split in two, and a huge red brightness leaped forward.

This is your new sun, Moon told Bear, naming the young and hungry baby. The sun was so hot it stole the sharpness of stone and the hardness of iron. Then came angry storms and fires that covered the world, so Moon quickly grabbed the red sun and jumped it into the sky.

Sky glances upward again, watching the nighttime darkness that named him. While Baby's voice settles, Sky's own story flicks to mind, of coming into the world unmoving and silent as Mother was dying, many summers ago. His deepest dreams still carry the sound of a woman's voice, but never a face or eyes. Instead, Sky's earliest memories are of a distant crying—Mark's, perhaps. He also remembers Green's strong hands and Tie's smiling teeth, but those memories came later. The day Sky was born his eyes only opened at the last minute, the ocean water startling his voice awake, almost too late, as he was being pushed out to sea with Mother's body.

The sky was the first thing you saw, Tie once told Sky, and it saved your life.

Teller, his body broken in the sand—it was Teller who saw Sky's eyes blinking open at the last moment, who looked for hope until the final instant. Teller, who needed the stories to be true, who dreamed of rescue and honored the others, naming the past to keep it alive.

And I didn't save him, thinks Sky miserably. In the end, the Enemy Ocean took Teller instead. Sky's voice, always late, did not open in time to save Teller.

Sky steadies the tremble in his throat, the cold guilt in his heart, to give Teller back his voice.

Moon still chases the sun, says Sky over Teller. Everyday their chase grows quicker, melting the days into one, bringing the heat closer. Sometimes Moon grows unhappy and so tired of the constant work. Sometimes Moon jumps from the sky and disappears in the tide pools, leaving everything behind—

Tie glances up, recognizing Green in these new words Sky has poured into the story. Sky hopes she recognizes Teller in these words, too, the way he held the group together with his voice, by threading their stories into the past.

Someday, continues Sky, the sun will move so slow and hot that whole lives will be spent between morning and evening, and at that time Moth will have no stars left to circle. That's when Moth and Bear will join together, and instead of us, Toad will sleep in the caves once more. Someday, when the Enemy Ocean and the sun eat each other, the world will be reborn through fire and flood. That's when Teller said all the old stories will begin again.

After a long silence filled only with the distant pound of the ocean waves chewing the beach, Sky takes hold of Teller's ankles and Mark hesitantly reaches for Teller's shoulders. Tie waves once, her fingers half-straightened, as they carry Teller down the dark sand dunes. After checking their foot wrappings, they cautiously cross the plastic-littered beach and the slippery rocks of low tide, until they settle Teller's body in the surf. Here we will feed him to the ocean, thinks Sky, the same ocean that swallowed Mother and Song and so many others, all returned to the largest cave to wait for the sun.

But even as the surf foams up around his kneeled body, Mark does not let go of Teller's hands. Sky has already stepped back, his palms filled forever with the touch of Teller's still skin, but Mark does not let go of Teller, his grip held fast, his words mumbled.

Can't, won't do it, don't want to—

And this, knows Sky, is how Mark holds grief, how Mother has been stored inside him for so long. Carefully, more full of care than he ever has been, Sky reaches for Mark's shoulder. Sky expects his hand to be knocked away, expects Mark to strike, but even as Mark tries to shrug off his touch, his clouded eyes remain wide, empty, and now incapable of anger. Slowly, Sky urges Mark away from Teller.

This isn't how he would want you to remember him, says Sky.

Will always remember him this way, says Mark, his blind hands trembling over Teller's face, brushing a crushed and silent mouth.

Sky frowns at the surf already pulling at Teller's legs.

You can remember more than this, says Sky.

Can't, repeats Mark. I can't, how? How—

But the questions release Mark's hands from Teller, his fingers clutching at nothing as he stands, his grief as hungry as the ocean.

I'll help, says Sky.

Mark drops his heavy arms over Sky's shoulders, leaning in his sobbing weight, his ear pressed into Sky's neck. Forgiveness, thinks Sky, as his arms wrap Mark's wide back and sorrow rises Mark's ribs into his. Family.

When Sky walks Mark back to the entrance of the cave tunnels, Tie is still watching with Baby sleeping in her arms, the ocean wind skimming over both their faces.

Teller, asks Tie, and Mark nods his face low.

A flash of inspiration, blue brilliance—the word Oh.

Stay here, says Sky, as he bounces back into the cave. In the darkness of the lower chambers, he shuffles his feet across the cracked floor, his toes kicking lightly against the kindling pile—no—the charcoal pile—no—and then Yes, his toes find it. He crouches to drag his fingers over the empty wooden shell, his other hand searching and finding the second half of the broken globe Mark found in the tide pools. One half is still sticky with Teller's blood, but both halves feel sure in Sky's hands—heavy and vital. Sky quickly fills the two bowls with flecks of kindling and flint, just like Egg must have held fire, and his legs fly him back up the sharp stairs to the cave entrance.

Pay attention, he says as he rushes past the others, out onto the sand dunes and running higher, making his way steadily across the headlands. His feet carry him over a path of burnt bricks and wedged stone, up a trail that narrows between the blackened basement of One, Two, Three—the house with one standing wall and three intact windows—and past the cliff edge at Three, Two, One—the hole where a house crumbled into the ocean in perfect thirds. The familiar path and wind-whipped structures keep Sky's piercing loneliness low, reminding him he is not far from home, not in this place where Green kept the last of his hopes, the sheer edge of the bluffs standing sharp against the sea.

At the brink of the cliff, Sky recognizes the collapsed foundations through hazy moonlight, the toothed concrete ringing the circular fire pit. The Observatory, he remembers—that's what Green called it. As Sky approaches the hollow, peeking over the lip, he squints to see chunks of ash lumped at the bottom of the crater, and slowly, next to long and jointed sticks, he makes out an unfurled pelvic bone, a blackened skull—the parts of Green beyond poison, living in fire. With a certainty that steadies Sky's trembling hands, he places the Egg halves near Green's remains, igniting a small streak of smoke and then a jumping flame.

Green believed in the bonfire more than anything, Teller once said, Teller who wanted Green and the bonfire to make the stories true. Stories—the spoken symbols of remembering. Not gifts from the gods, but words to remind us of what was, to connect me to myself, my name, my memory that can Save Us with sounds and scratches of language, protecting the past and present and my family— Mark, Tie, and Baby watching from the caves below.

The fire leaps and spirals in the wind, lashing its pale smoke upward, into the stars that might be watching. Moon, Mars, Venus, and Moth—if they exist, they might be observing, might know I'm here. Beyond the cliffs is the Enemy Ocean, an ongoing horizon broken only by the remains of Old City. The single building has been knawed to its steel frames, driven open by the summer storms— so many hundreds of terrible storms—but three stars peer brightly through the square bones. Three stars, and then four, the fourth star moving steadily across the others, blinking and Radiant—a Walking Star journeying through the night. A Walking Star, or perhaps Moth itself, drifting overhead until the time comes, as sparks from the fire perish in shadow and flare once more, flashes of light thrown upward and remembered, while the darkness everywhere waits for the stories to begin again.

ACKNOWLEDGMENTS

There's a river near where I grew up and every spring, when the water level is highest, people dare each other to jump off the bridges into the river far below. Writing *From the Caves* was somewhat similar, I think—a jump away, a plunge towards. I want to thank my friends and family who waved from the bridge when I moved to Oregon to return to writing, as well as the people who hailed me from the riverbanks: my peers and mentors at Portland State University, my fellow writers at the 2015 Tin House Summer Workshop, *pacificREVIEW* for anthologizing the first chapter, and the editors and novella contest judges at Red Hen Press. I also want to thank the people who were midair with me throughout the writing process: the many wonderful readers who discussed my early and later drafts in classrooms and living rooms, especially my husband, who was suspended with me the entire time and in many ways. Matt, I am so grateful for our conversations on writing, your saintly patience, and your unyielding support these last few years.

BIOGRAPHICAL NOTE

Thea Prieto is a recipient of the Laurels Award Fellowship as well as a finalist for the international Edwin L. Stockton, Jr. Award and *Glimmer Train*'s Short Story Award for New Writers. She writes and edits for *Poets & Writers*, *Propeller Magazine*, and *The Gravity of the Thing*, and her work has also appeared at *New Orleans Review*, *Longreads*, *Entropy*, *The Masters Review*, and elsewhere. She lives in Portland, Oregon, where she teaches creative writing at Portland State University and Portland Community College. *From the Caves* is her first book.